# PERSONAL BEST

## BY MARGARET WATSON

ISBN-13: 978-1497451551

# DEDICATION

For Bill, my love.

# TITLES BY MARGARET WATSON

Find Me (Donovan Family Series)
Watch Me (Donovan Family Series)
Love Me (Donovan Family Series)
Bending the Rules
The Woman He Knows
A Safe Place
For Baby and Me
Life Rewritten
Can't Stand the Heat
An Unlikely Setup
Home at Last
No Place like Home
A Place Called Home
Stranger in a Small Town
Small-Town Family
Small-Town Secrets
Family First
In Her Defense
Hometown Girl
Two on the Run
To Love and Protect Her
Someone to Watch over Her
A Thanksgiving to Remember
Family on the Run
The Marriage Protection Program
The Fugitive Bride
Cowboy with a Badge
For the Children
Rodeo Man
The Dark Side of the Moon
To Save his Child
An Honorable Man
An Innocent Man
Personal Best

# NOTE TO MY READERS

Personal Best was the first book I published, back in 1991. People have been asking for years where they could get a copy, so I decided to make it available again. I'm very proud of this book, but as I read it over, I saw it for what it is – a book from 1991. So many things have changed since then, technology most of all. There were no cell phones back then. It was the early days of personal computers, and not everyone had one. The Chicago Marathon was far different than it is today, and recycling has become the norm, rather than a new and exciting option which was pioneered by individuals rather than cities. I still remember hauling our recyclables to a collection center several miles from our home.

So as you read Personal Best, please remember that it was a different world when it was written. I debated updating it, but finally decided that it was more fun to leave it as it was written, so we can all appreciate how much our world has changed.

# CHAPTER ONE

Tess Phillips's legs screamed each time her feet hit the pavement. She felt each individual muscle protest as her leg stretched, then contracted again. Forcing her mind to ignore the pain in her legs, Tess concentrated instead on her feet. One toe had begun to rub on her sock and for a moment all feeling focused on that point. She closed her eyes and squeezed away the pain, willing herself to ignore the forming blister.

The noise of the spectators echoed in her ears and Tess opened her eyes. Their rhythmic clapping and shouting echoed the slap of her feet on the pavement. She still had three miles to go until the end of the race, and she was amazed at the hundreds of people who lined the street. They were all yelling encouragement at the runners, the individual voices blending into a continuous stream of sound that pulled her along. The cheers spurred her on and helped her ignore the now constant pain.

One more mile to go. Her lungs were on fire. Every breath she took was a searing pain ripping through her chest. She wiped the sweat off her forehead, and realized that her arm was trembling. Her legs were shaking, too, but she forced herself to ignore them. Up ahead she saw the last water stand. "Got to have some Gatorade there," she mumbled to herself. She knew that if she didn't get

1

some sugar, she wouldn't be able to finish the race. She swerved by the table, and without breaking stride grabbed a glass of the sweet green liquid. Drinking it greedily as she ran, she noticed the difference immediately. Energy flowed into her muscles, strength gathered again in her legs.

The roar of the spectators thundered around her. The pack of men she had been running with had all either surged ahead or fallen behind, and now she was running alone. She heard the shouts and even sometimes the individual voices, but still no words broke through her haze.

Suddenly a young man stepped off the curb and yelled "Water?" directly at her, and she nodded gratefully. The next instant a cup of cool water splashed over her head. The droplets cascaded down her face and dripped onto her shirt. It was heaven.

Tess turned off Lake Shore Drive and headed for Cannon Drive. The finish line was less than a half mile away. As she started up the short stretch of road that led to Cannon Drive, a surge of adrenaline hit her and her rubbery muscles began pumping furiously. She was almost there! All the months of preparation hadn't prepared her for the brutal reality of the race, but her pain fell away as she neared the corner of Cannon Drive. The familiar surge of anticipation as the finish line approached made her feet move a little more quickly.

She turned the corner and finally saw the finish line a quarter of a mile away. There were thousands of people lining both sides of the drive, and when they saw her start down the street a tremendous, deafening roar arose. The sound rolled toward her and seemed to pick her up and carry her forward.

Tess turned to look at the crowd in awe, and when she looked back at the finish line, she saw two race officials stretching a banner across it. For a moment she stared, uncomprehending. Then suddenly she understood—there were no women runners ahead of her. The tape was for her! Her feet faltered momentarily, then picked up speed and flew across the pavement. She was going to be the first woman to cross the finish line at this marathon!

Tess couldn't feel her legs anymore. She couldn't breathe. She could only hear the thundering, continuous noise from the crowd as it echoed around her. She could only see the tape at the finish line as it came closer and closer. Finally the thin strip of paper pressed against her chest and snapped, and she stumbled for a few more steps before strong arms grabbed her and held her upright.

Someone wrapped what looked like a huge piece of aluminum foil around her. She swayed for a few moments, supported by gentle arms, sucking in huge gulps of air.

A young man handed her a glass of water, and she let a small stream of liquid dribble into her mouth. A smiling woman passed her a towel, and Tess wiped the sweat off her face and neck. She stood for a moment holding the towel over her face, trembling and gasping for breath.

She looked around, dazed and disoriented. She had wrapped herself in a shell of concentration during the race, and it had just begun to crack. Only now did she begin to notice her surroundings. It seemed like there were thousands of people pressing in on her, surging toward her, all pushing and shoving. Suddenly one man came forward and took her arm.

"Miss Phillips, I'm Roger Hayward, the president of the Chicago Marathon, and I want to be the first to congratulate you on your victory." The short, balding man licked his lips nervously and looked around, as if he were afraid of what he might see.

"Normally, Miss Phillips, we would now escort you to the podium for the awards ceremony, but we have a little problem today." He looked around again, and Tess opened her mouth to ask what was wrong, when he continued with a rush, "Because of the unusual circumstances of the finish today, the reporters are demanding to speak to you immediately. I'm afraid that I won't be able to get you to the podium until you answer their questions."

Tess took another shuddering breath and opened her mouth to speak. When no words came out, she took another drink of water and cleared her throat. "Mr. Hayward, what was so unusual about the finish of this race?" Her voice was harsh and raspy and totally alien to her ears.

Roger Hayward swallowed a few times and said quickly, "The fact that an unknown was the winner of the women's race. There are some world class women running today, and nobody has ever heard of you. All these reporters carry computers with them, you know, and they can't find any information about your previous marathon times." He looked at her almost accusingly, as if she were deliberately keeping this important information from him.

Tess shifted her weight to keep her quivering legs from collapsing beneath her. "I don't have any previous times. This is my first marathon."

Hayward's eyes widened, and he just stared at her for a moment. Then he sighed. "All right, I'll postpone the awards ceremony. When these reporters hear that, they're going to be all over you like starving dogs on a bone."

Once the decision had been made, Hayward seemed to lose his nervousness and took control. "I'll stay here with you, and after a few questions I can escort you to the stand."

He turned to the crowd of reporters that pressed closer. "All right, ladies and gentlemen, Miss Phillips will answer a few of your questions before we proceed with the ceremony."

Tess's already flushed face grew even redder. She hadn't agreed to answer any questions. No way could she cope with this pack of reporters when all she wanted was to sit down. Her legs felt like wet spaghetti, and her shoes were at least three sizes too small. Then she looked around, and the reality of the situation hit her.

She had just won the Chicago Marathon, beating a number of internationally known women runners. Women who had competed in the Olympics, who had won other major marathons. Women who were supposed to have won this marathon. No wonder Mr. Hayward seemed nervous. The sports writers had probably been hounding him unmercifully for the last fifteen minutes. Gathering her nerve, she forced herself to look out at the reporters, and they immediately began shouting questions at her. She heard the sound of innumerable cameras clicking. Technicians waved microphones at her as the reporters surged even closer. Tess fought to remain standing as her legs wobbled and shook beneath her.

"Miss Phillips!" someone shouted. "What other marathons have you run in, and was your time today a personal best?"

"This was my first marathon," Tess answered, her voice as shaky as her legs. She almost pinched herself to make sure she wasn't dreaming. Was this really happening to her?

"Are you saying you've never run a marathon before today?" an incredulous voice asked.

"That's right," Tess answered, trying not to sound so breathless.

"Who's your coach?" someone else called out.

"I don't have a coach, I train by myself," Tess replied.

Tess had been scanning the group of reporters as she answered their questions, but her eyes kept going back to one man in particular. He stood at the back of the group, and as far as she could tell he was the only person there who wasn't either recording her words or taking notes. Instead, he simply stood there, watching her. She wasn't sure if he was a reporter or just an interested bystander, but she couldn't prevent her eyes from continually returning to his face.

He was a tall man. Even standing at the back of the crowd, he was able to look directly at her. His dark hair curled over his collar, and although she couldn't tell the color of his eyes from a distance, she could feel their intensity.

She deliberately looked away from him as she answered another question. Even as she concentrated on a woman standing close to her, listening to her words, she could feel the man's eyes still fixed on her. She couldn't prevent herself from glancing at him again, and was surprised to see a faint smile pass over his face as their eyes met. It wasn't a pleasant smile, either. It reminded her of the way the nuns in grade school used to look when Tess had been caught red-handed in some escapade.

Just then Roger Hayward spoke up. "Thank you, ladies and gentlemen. We're going to proceed with the awards ceremony now, and then I'm sure Miss Phillips will be glad to answer any further questions."

In a pig's eye, Tess said to herself as Hayward led her up the stairs. She had already answered all possible questions at least twice. All she wanted now was to go home and soak in her bathtub for at least two days.

"Congratulations, Miss Phillips," a woman said, and it echoed from all sides as everyone on the stand reached out to shake her hand.

"Nice job," said a man in a white warm up suit. Tess reached out to shake his hand, and realized that this must be the winner of the men's race. His jacket was covered with the insignia of numerous sports equipment and clothing manufacturers. "Congratulations to you, too," she answered.

The man smiled and said, "I know that this is your first time up here. It's a bit intimidating, isn't it?" He had a slight Spanish accent, and Tess recognized him as the runner who had been favored to win the men's division, a South American who had represented his country in the last Olympics.

Tess looked around at the crowds, still not sure she wasn't dreaming. She'd won more than her share of races, but that was a long time ago, in what seemed like a different life. The Chicago Marathon was in another class altogether. She sighed. Maybe there was more of her uncle in her than she was prepared to acknowledge. That fierce competitiveness that had pushed her to train to her absolute limits had to come from somewhere. In spite of everything that had happened between them, she wished he was here today.

Her feeling of unreality grew as an official presented her with a trophy and placed a circle of leaves on her head. She looked out at the crowd, and found herself searching through the group of reporters. With a pang of disappointment, she realized that the tall, dark-haired man was gone. Her eyes scanned the throngs surrounding the platform, but he had disappeared.

Get a grip on yourself, Tess, she admonished herself. Since when do you stand around mooning about some guy you see in a crowd? Especially since he didn't seem to be any great admirer of yours, her saner self reminded her.

She forced her wandering attention back to the events on the platform. One of the officials finished speaking, and handed her a piece of paper. It was a check, and when Tess looked at it she had to make a conscious effort to keep her mouth from dropping open. Slowly she raised her eyes to stare at the official, but he was presenting a check to the smiling man opposite her.

Tess stood in a daze and listened to the rest of the speeches. She thought she received numerous prizes of sports equipment, food and beverages from the various sponsors of the race, but her mind was numb. Finally, after what seemed like hours, the spectators started clapping and she realized that the ceremony was over.

Hesitating, she turned to look around, not sure what to do next, and her eyes met the dark-haired man's again. This time, she didn't look away, and as they stared at each other an almost visible current crackled between them. The man made an abrupt movement toward her, and the spell was broken.

Glancing toward the steps of the platform, she somehow expected to see the man magically appear. What she saw instead was her roommate Donna, along with three of her other friends, all grinning and shouting at her. By the time the four women finished hugging and congratulating her, they had moved away from the throng of people and were walking across the grass toward Donna's car.

Tess couldn't stop herself from looking back over her shoulder once before getting into the back seat. Disappointed, she sank back into the worn upholstery and closed her eyes. Over the hum of the engine and the excited comments of her friends, she could see with startling clarity those intense eyes staring at her and that mocking grin curling his lips. Hey, he's not your type anyway, she reminded herself. It was just too bad, a niggling little voice said, that you won't have the chance to find out for yourself.

\*\*\*

"No way!" Nick Bartholomew glared at his editor, jumped up, and paced across the room. Art McArney leaned back in his chair and watched Nick, raising one eyebrow.

"Come on, Arnie, use some logic: This was the Chicago Marathon. No way could someone without a hell of a lot of marathon experience win that race. There were at least five women running who were either former winners or heavy favorites to win. This Phillips woman comes out of nowhere, beats the next closest woman by a full minute, then calmly tells us that she's never run a marathon before, let alone won one. What else can I think except that she's got some scam going?"

"Then why don't you want to do this story?" The editor watched him for a moment. "Talk to me, Bartholomew. This is supposed to be your thing, exposing sports scams. I'd've thought you'd want to stick to this broad like a cheap shirt." He leaned forward in his chair. "For that matter, how do you know she's hustling anybody? For someone who's trying to pull a fast one, she's keeping a very low profile."

Nick threw himself onto the couch along the wall. "I'm sure it's all part of the bigger picture. Whet the press's appetite, stir up interest by not giving interviews—she seems like a master at the game."

Nick jumped up again and strode over to his editor's desk. "Mark my words, Arnie, by doing this feature on her, we're playing right into her hands. I, for one, refuse to give her the publicity she so obviously wants. Find someone else to do this piece."

Arnie burrowed through his desk drawer, searching. Finally, with a satisfied grunt, he leaned back in his chair and lit a huge cigar. He rolled the cigar around in his mouth, savoring the flavor. Narrowing his eyes, he looked at Nick.

"So what's the problem? You'll have a week with the woman. Of all the people I've got, you're the one who's most likely to figure out what her angle is. If you can't nail Tess Phillips, nobody can."

"I just don't like it, Arnie. I don't like her and I don't like whatever her angle is."

Nick leaned against Arnie's desk, not quite meeting his editor's eyes. That wasn't exactly the whole reason, and he suspected Arnie knew it. The problem was Tess Phillips had intrigued him from the moment he'd seen her stumble across the finish line at Sunday's race. He had watched her at the impromptu press conference right afterwards, and had been reluctantly impressed by her cool, in-control facade. And by a lot more than that, he admitted to himself. Each time her eyes had met his, he'd felt a little jolt. Knowing that she must be a phony, he didn't want any part of this assignment. He wasn't going to take any chances. No female athlete was going to get close to him and then use him again.

"You know, Nick, just because the girl is attractive and an athlete doesn't mean she's another Vicky Chessman." Arnie watched him carefully.

Nick's face darkened as he glared at his editor. Arnie didn't miss much. Damn him, anyway.

"Vicky has nothing to do with this. That's ancient history."

Arnie gave him a quizzical look. "I don't know, you seem awfully set against this Phillips woman. You haven't even heard her story yet. Could the old saw about 'once burned, twice shy' have anything to do with that?"

"I repeat, anything that happened with Vicky Chessman is completely irrelevant." Nick looked away. Arnie sometimes had an uncanny ability to read his mind. Regardless of his personal feelings, though, Nick knew he was right on this one.

Arnie raised one eyebrow. "Haven't you even considered the possibility that this Phillips woman is telling the truth?"

"For about a second. Arnie, something like that's never been done before. It's like an unknown colt winning the Kentucky Derby by twenty lengths. It's possible, but not real likely."

Arnie sat up in his chair decisively. "Well, then, this has all the makings of a great story. 'Nick Bartholomew exposes another sports scandal.' Probably a Pulitzer in it for you." He bent over his desk as if suddenly busy. After a minute he looked up. "You still here, Bartholomew?" He gave Nick a steely gaze.

"Arnie," Nick began angrily, then paused in the doorway as the editor gave him a warning look. "Why don't you invest in a classier cigar? Those things smell like something that died last week," he finished mildly. Before

Arnie had time to reply, Nick quietly closed the door.

Back in the city room, he stopped for a moment and scanned the commotion. Telephones jangled, men and women pounded computer keyboards and the atmosphere was one of barely controlled chaos. He stormed over to his desk and slammed into his chair.

"What's the problem, Bartholomew?" someone called. Nick looked up at the face of Jim Krieg. "Arnie not being properly respectful of your genius?" Nick scowled back at the young reporter, who laughed and said, "What'd he do, tell you to cover the high school golf action?"

Nick's lips twitched as he leaned back and picked up his coffee cup. "Worse. I have to spend the next week with Ms. Tess Phillips, that woman who won the Chicago Marathon."

Nick took a sip of his coffee and grimaced. "One of the major benefits of working for this newspaper is that your coffee is always cold. Makes it easy to cut back." He set the cup back on his desk and looked at Jim, who was staring at him.

"You aren't really saying what I think you're saying, are you?" Jim asked incredulously.

"What do you mean?"

"You're telling me that you don't want to spend a week with Tess Phillips? That you actually would rather interview smelly football players than that gorgeous creature?" Jim shook his head. "Boy, whatever's in that coffee, I'm staying away from it."

Nick shook his head. "Hey, if that were all there was to it, I'd have been there yesterday." He tried, unsuccessfully, to push Tess's image out of his head. "The thing is, Jim, I'm sure that publicity is just what she wants. It makes me furious that the paper is going to play her game, and even angrier that I have to be the one to do it."

"But how do you know that she is playing games? Maybe this really was her first marathon. If it was, it's a hell of a story."

Nick sighed. "Yes, Jim, it is possible. It's also possible that pigs will fly someday, too, but not anytime soon." Nick leaned back in his chair. "Do you know how much money she won in that race Sunday? Fifty thousand dollars."

He smiled grimly as Jim whistled. "Yeah, a hell of a lot of money. Do you know how much more she stands to make from endorsements? The whole set up is just too damned perfect." Nick slammed the chair back to the floor angrily. "She's the advertiser's dream come true. Drop dead gorgeous, great body, and she just won a major U.S. road race. Never even ran a marathon before, either. The poor suckers will be standing in line with bushel baskets full of money just to get her name on their products. Yeah, a perfect set up, as far as Ms. Phillips is concerned."

"And you think that your columns will just give her the publicity she wants," Jim said slowly

Nick smiled. "Oh, they'll give her publicity, all right. Whether it's the kind she wants or not is another story."

Jim laughed again as he walked away. "I can't wait to read these columns, Nick. Just watch your step with the lovely Ms. Phillips. We wouldn't want you to lose your famous, um, objectivity."

Nick grinned at Jim's retreating back. It was true, he never had been noted for his objective viewpoint. One of the things that drew readers to his column was his outspoken taking of sides. And he was certainly not going to let this unfortunate ...attraction to Tess Phillips blind him to what she was trying to do.

Once again, Tess's image appeared before his eyes. Damn the woman, anyway. For the last two days, he had been obsessed with her. It was that last look over her shoulder as she was getting into the car that had done it. It was almost as if she were looking for him. Then with a flash of long, smooth leg she was gone. Ever since, every time he caught a glimpse of a woman with a long blond braid, his heartbeat quickened.

Nick sat up decisively. Well, he was going to get to the truth about Tess Phillips in record time. Then he could forget all about her. He hoped.

\*\*\*

"You've got to be kidding!" Tess looked at her friend and sometimes roommate Donna Parker incredulously. "There's no way I'm going to let some reporter follow me around for a week."

Tess plopped the bag of groceries on the table and slipped her purse onto a chair. "What exactly did he say, anyway? I'm sure he didn't just tell you he was going to be here this afternoon. No one, not even a reporter, could be that rude."

Donna shook her head. "That's what he said, all right. He would be here this afternoon to start talking to you for the story."

"Well, I hope you set him straight," Tess shot back.

Donna sat down in a kitchen chair. "As a matter of fact, I did mention to Mr. Bartholomew that he might want to talk to you before making any final arrangements. He seemed to think it wouldn't be necessary."

Tess's stomach began to flutter. "All right, Donna, what's going on?"

"Well, Tess, it seems that when you entered the Marathon, you signed an entry form. That entry form said that, if you won, the Chicago Post had the rights to your story. Specifically, the Post can assign a reporter to you for up to a week."

"I don't want to be dissected in the Chicago Post or any other newspaper," Tess exclaimed hotly. "He can just take his tape recorder and notepad and stuff them!"

Donna laughed. "Hey, don't take it so hard. The guy's a gorgeous hunk, you know."

"What guy?"

13

"Nick Bartholomew, the man who called."

"I don't care if he's the second coming of Paul Newman. No one's going to take me apart for public consumption." Tess paused and gave Donna a calculating look. "And just how do you know what he looks like, anyway?"

"Oh," Donna waved her hand airily, "I saw him one afternoon on one of those sports writers' talk shows. You know, the ones where there are five or six men chewing on cigars, all talking at once about some hot sports topic."

"Donna," Tess asked with real interest, "when did you start watching sports talk shows?"

"It was just a show that Paul was watching once, and I got interested."

"You don't even know the difference between a football and a baseball. Since when are you interested in a sportswriters' show?" Tess had almost forgotten about the original reason for their discussion, she was so intrigued. Donna's fiance, Paul, was mildly interested in sports, but she just couldn't picture the two of them watching a sports talk show.

Donna grinned conspiratorially. "Paul was pretty surprised, too. He was watching this program when I walked in, and one of the guys on the panel caught my eye. He was so smooth, and so good looking, that I had to find out who it was. And guess what?"

"It was Nick Bartholomew," Tess finished disgustedly. "Donna, just because you have the hots for this guy doesn't mean I have to put up with him for a week."

"Tess! I'm an engaged woman, and the only person I have the hots for is Paul. That doesn't mean I can't appreciate what I see." Donna gave Tess a measuring look. "And maybe think my friend would appreciate it, too."

Tess had to laugh. At least Donna was upfront about her motives. And that was the trouble with people who were in love. They couldn't stand to see anyone who wasn't in the same condition. "Donna, I do appreciate your concern. The last thing I want right now, though, is to get involved with anyone, and especially with some reporter who's supposed to strip me naked for a newspaper column." She stood up and began to put the groceries away. "Really, tell me what he said. When is he supposed to call me back?"

"You think I'm joking, don't you?" Donna's smile faded. "Honestly, Tess, Nick Bartholomew is coming over here this afternoon, and I got the distinct impression that he's planning to be here for a while."

Tess whirled angrily on Donna. "Who does he think he is, anyway? I may have signed that entry form, and believe me I'm going to check it, but that doesn't mean that Mr. Nick Bartholomew can just waltz in here any time he feels like it."

"I did tell him that you wouldn't be too pleased, but he didn't seem to believe me. He just laughed and said to tell you to have your story ready." Donna sounded unhappy. "Actually, Tess, he may be a handsome hunk, but he sounded pretty unpleasant on the phone."

Tess stared at Donna for a moment, thinking. "Let me get my copy of the entry form," she said slowly. "I want to see what I signed." She hurried to the desk in her office, returning a minute later with a paper in her hand.

"It says here," Tess scanned the page, "that in the event I win either the men's or women's division of the race the Chicago Post has sole and exclusive rights to my story. I can't talk to any other newspaper, magazine, or any other publication for at least a month after the race." She looked up at Donna. "Well, that's easy. They can print my story. I ran the marathon, I won the marathon. I'm certainly not going to let anybody else interview me, so that should fulfill my obligation nicely."

"Are you sure that form doesn't say anything else?" Donna asked dubiously.

Tess looked at the paper again, and felt her stomach

twist. "There is the little matter of the prize money. If I refuse the interview, the money is forfeited." Tess raised stricken eyes to Donna. "There's no way that the recycling center can survive without that money, Donna. We've already spent most of it."

Donna nodded unhappily. "I know, Tess. I work there, too, remember?"

Tess threw herself down into a chair and looked around her living room. "I can't bear the thought of some stranger coming in here and poking through my life. It would feel like such a violation." She stared around the room without really seeing it. Besides that, she thought, there was the matter of her business. She and a partner operated a small recycling center in their suburb. For the past few months it had been steadily losing money. If this reporter was going to be shadowing her for any length of time, her business would be part of the story.

Tess sighed and leaned back on the couch. It would be the perfect angle for a story, she knew. "Marathon winner desperately needs prize money to keep company afloat. Check arrives just in time." What reporter, she thought with a sneer, could resist.

Once the suburbs around here knew that the Greener Earth Recycling Center was having problems, they wouldn't be likely to sign contracts for new routes. Who was going to do business with a company sliding into bankruptcy? They would run, not walk, to Tess's competition, the giant Recovery Services, Inc. And without new routes, the Greener Earth wouldn't have the volume they needed to make a profit. It was a perfect Catch 22. If she accepted the prize money, she had to let this reporter do the story, and there was a good chance that it would accelerate the crash of the recycling center. If she gave back the fifty thousand dollars, the center would fold for sure.

"I guess I have no choice but to talk to this guy," Tess said wearily. "But there is no way he's going to write anything about my personal life or the center. He can write all he wants about how I train, what clothes I wear, or what shoes I prefer. But that's it."

"Tess, that might be easier said than done," Donna said softly.

Tess jumped up and set her chin. "We'll see, Donna. We'll just see."

She turned around and marched into her bedroom and slammed the door. A few minutes later she emerged, dressed in sweatpants and running shoes.

"Um, where are you going, Tess? Nick Bartholomew should be here any time."

"I'm going for a run, Donna. A nice, long run," Tess answered sweetly. "If Mr. Bartholomew arrives while I'm gone, just ask him to wait."

Tess let the screen door bang behind her as she started running. It might be a small victory in the preliminary skirmish, but she was determined to savor it.

# CHAPTER TWO

Thirty-five minutes. Tess looked up from her watch with satisfaction. She'd been afraid that she wouldn't be able to handle her usual forty-five minute run only three days after the marathon. Only ten minutes from home, though, and she felt just fine. The rhythmic thud of her feet on the pavement echoed her shallow breathing. The cool air felt like silk caressing her bare legs. The regular slap of her braid on her back blended with all the other familiar sensations of running and, like always, she felt her mind clearing.

Tess turned the corner onto her own street. She was several blocks away from her house, but she lengthened her stride and started to sprint. She liked to finish with a flourish, and she always ran the last blocks at full speed.

As she neared the first house on her block, she passed a car parked at the curb. She didn't even glance at it as she sped by. Suddenly, in a blur of motion, there was a man running beside her. Tess was so startled that she stumbled to a halt as she turned to look at him.

"Please don't stop on my account, Ms. Phillips," a deep voice said smoothly. "I've been looking forward to observing your style a little more closely."

All she could do was stare. It was the tall, dark-haired man from the race on Sunday. A man, she remembered with a blush, that she had wondered about more than once in the past two days. Tess looked up at his face. His deep blue eyes, prominent nose and cheekbones and wavy dark brown hair looked even better in person than in her imagination. Thank goodness, her face was already flushed from running!

"Who are you and what are you doing here?" Tess asked, retreating a step.

"Didn't your roommate tell you that I was coming?" The man looked puzzled, as if it was the most natural thing in the world for him to be there.

An awful feeling settled in the pit of her stomach. "You're Nick Bartholomew, aren't you?"

He smiled pleasantly. "In person. Pleased to meet you, Ms. Phillips." He held out his hand, and after only a momentary hesitation, Tess held out her own.

Nick slid his warm, dry palm against her hot and sweaty one. Tess gave his hand a firm squeeze, then slowly unclasped her fingers. She had never realized how intimate a handshake could be. In that brief moment, all sorts of messages passed between her and Nick Bartholomew, unspoken but nevertheless crystal clear.

Nick stared at her as if she'd suddenly sprouted two heads, and Tess suspected she looked equally astonished. Never in her wildest nightmares had she imagined that her fantasy man from the race would turn out to be the reporter she already resented. She was even more astounded by the all too obvious current that had flowed between them just now.

"Excuse me." Tess took a step backward, as if physical distance was her only hope of safety. "I haven't quite finished my run. I'll be back soon." She turned and started running again, hoping that Nick wouldn't see her retreat as the escape it was. Hearing footsteps coming up alongside her, Tess turned her head and wasn't really surprised to see Nick jogging along easily beside her.

"You don't mind if I come with you, do you?" He

smiled innocently, and Tess gritted her teeth.

"I don't like to talk while I'm running, Mr. Bartholomew," she said pointedly.

"No problem. We have all week to talk. Right now we'll just run."

\*\*\*

They ran on in silence as Tess fumed. She really hated running with anybody else, especially someone who'd invited himself along. They passed her house all too quickly, and she thought longingly of her warm shower and dry clothes. She couldn't very well stop now, though, after making an issue of wanting to continue her workout. She sneaked a glance at her watch. Ten minutes more, fifteen tops, was really all she should run today. She didn't want to overdo it so soon after the marathon. Ten minutes, she decided, would be enough. She plotted out a course in her mind, and settled into a steady rhythm

She glanced at Nick. He seemed perfectly at ease, relaxed even, and actually looked as if he was enjoying himself. He was very tall, towering over her five feet eight inches. His worn, red T-shirt and navy blue sweat pants emphasized his broad shoulders and slim waist and hips. Tess sighed. She had to admit, Donna had been right about the gorgeous hunk part of her description.

Used to running by herself, Tess found it unnerving to have someone running steadily along beside her. She tried changing speed, but Nick adjusted to the faster pace effortlessly. She slowed down, and again, without any apparent effort, he readjusted. Frustrated, she suddenly sprinted ahead at full speed.

For a moment, Tess smiled in triumph. Nick was still behind her. Then she heard the relentless pounding of his shoes on the pavement, and he was next to her again. She didn't dare look at him. She just kept going, arms and legs pumping furiously, as she headed for home.

Nick was still matching her, stride for stride, as they turned into her driveway. Tess slowed to a walk and finally turned to look at him. At least he was breathing as heavily as she was. Catching her eye, he smiled sardonically at her. "Do you always finish your runs with a two mile sprint?"

Tess avoided looking at him. "Most of the time." She glanced at him then as he eased himself down onto the ground. He collapsed against a tree, threw back his head and gulped in air. In spite of herself, she grinned. "Especially when I'm running with a reporter who thinks he's hot stuff."

Nick lowered his head at that and looked at her. To her surprise, a genuine smile appeared on his face, and he burst out laughing. "Touche, Ms. Phillips. I suppose I deserved that. Can we consider ourselves even?"

Still smiling, she said, "Since you've apologized so nicely, the incident is forgotten."

She sat down on the ground opposite him and leaned against the fence, still breathing hard. "There aren't too many people who could have kept up that pace. Are you a runner?"

Nick shook his head. "Not in your class, that's for sure." Tess thought he gave her an odd, measuring look, but it was gone almost instantly. "I played basketball in college, and got into the habit of running then. Now, I guess you could say I'm a recreational runner. I do it to stay in shape, but that's all."

A cool breeze blew against Tess's damp shirt, making her shiver. "We'd better go inside. It's too chilly to be sitting out here today." She jumped up and waited for Nick to rise more slowly. "I'm getting cold."

Tess glanced at Nick as they walked toward the house. Why, oh why did Nick Bartholomew have to turn out to be her mystery man from the race? Her cheeks flushed red again as she remembered her fantasies about him during the past three days. Nick was the reporter who was going to interview her, to probe into her life and try to ferret out her secrets. The enemy. Why couldn't he have been someone she could just dismiss from her mind and forget? Tess sighed. One thing she was sure of, she wasn't going to be able to forget Nick Bartholomew.

"I'm back, Donna," she called as they walked into the living room.

She heard the creak of a chair, and Donna came bounding out of her bedroom. "Hey, before you get comfortable, I've got to warn you," she began. Then she spotted Nick standing next to Tess. "Oh," she said weakly, "I see you've met."

"Donna," Tess said stiffly, "this is Nick Bartholomew. Nick, this is my roommate, Donna Parker."

"I know." Donna said faintly. "We, ah, met earlier, while you were still running."

"Oh, good." Tess ran her fingers down her braid in a quick, nervous gesture. She glanced at her sweatpants and sweatshirt. They were beginning to feel clammy, cold, and definitely uncomfortable. "Donna, were you planning on going anywhere?"

"Not for a while. Why?"

"I'd like to take a shower," Tess muttered. Maybe a few minutes alone would help her regain her composure. She glanced at Nick, then back at Donna.

"Feel free, Ms. Phillips. My time is yours," Nick said gallantly, with only a hint of a smile.

Tess looked again at Nick as Donna said, "Sure, I'll stick around for a while. Go ahead."

As Tess shut her bedroom door, she heard Donna say breezily, "Have a seat, Nick. Can I get you a soda or anything?"

Nick prowled the small living room. He could hear the shower running behind the thin wall, and he imagined Tess standing in the warm water, letting it wash the sweat and stiffness out of her. With an oath, he threw his long frame onto her couch. This was going to be a damn rough week,

22

if the last half hour was any indication.

He had been prepared, he thought, to meet Tess Phillips. Blocking her beauty out of his mind, he'd concentrated instead on her probable dishonesty. What he hadn't been prepared for was the sledgehammer that had hit him when he'd shaken her hand. A blow that had struck Tess, too, if her face was any indication.

Damn it to hell. He didn't want to like Tess Phillips. He was even less prepared to acknowledge the electricity he felt whenever he looked at her. This was a woman, he tried to tell himself, who represented everything dirty and demeaning about sports, everything he'd spent his career trying to expose. A woman who was looking for nothing but publicity and a fast buck. In spite of himself, though, he could see every detail of her face as if she were standing in front of him. Her long hair, pulled back into a single braid, was ten different shades of blond. Her huge eyes were so blue and clear that a person could lose themselves in their depths and not surface for days. And her body. Nick shifted uncomfortably as he imagined what Tess looked like beneath her baggy sweatpants and sweatshirt. Yeah, it was going to be one hell of a week.

Donna reappeared in the living room and sat down in a chair opposite him. Setting the cans of cola on the table, she leaned back and smiled.

"So, Nick, how's the newspaper biz?"

They exchanged small talk for a few minutes, then fell silent. Finally, Nick said, "If you have something else to do, go right ahead. You really don't have to sit here and guard me, you know. I can behave myself while Tess is in the shower."

Donna gave him an appraising look, then grinned. "I guess that's Tess's loss, isn't it?"

Nick's answering grin faded as Donna disappeared into her room. He looked around the living room of the small house. You could tell a lot about a person from their home, he thought. The couch he sat on was comfortable and inviting, just like the rest of the room. It was covered in a flowered fabric, and two afghans rested on its back. A contemporary rug in vivid, bold colors covered the hardwood floor. It should have clashed with the soft pastels of the upholstery, but somehow they fit together perfectly. In one corner stood two bookcases, full of well thumbed books. Someone liked paintings, Nick thought, as he looked at the watercolors and oils on the walls. They were all different scenes and different styles, but again they looked as if they belonged together. Yeah, a comfortable room.

The sound of the shower stopped and Nick heard Tess moving around in her bedroom. He heard the low whine of a hair dryer, and his muscles tensed as he pictured Tess's hair blowing around her face and shoulders. Disgusted with himself, he jumped up and stormed outside. Maybe he could concentrate on his strategy for the interviews if he wasn't so distracted. Nick took his notebook out of the pocket of his sweatpants, but instead of writing down incisive, blunt questions, he simply stared at the blank pages, his mind wandering elsewhere.

Tess opened her bedroom door and took a few tentative steps into the living room. Hope soared as she saw it was empty. Don't be an idiot, she told herself wearily. Just because you wished he would vanish from the face of the earth doesn't mean he's gone. She wandered into the kitchen, and caught sight of Nick in the backyard. He was standing there, just staring at the back of the house. Tess gathered her courage, took a deep breath, and walked out the door.

"Hello, Mr. Bartholomew. Aren't you a little cold out here, especially after working up a sweat?"

"No, actually, I was a little, ah, warm inside," Nick answered blandly.

"Well, why don't you come back into the house and we can get this interview over with."

Nick narrowed his eyes at that as he walked past her

into the kitchen. Looking around until he spotted the wastebasket, he tossed his empty cola can into the container. As he moved into the living room, out of the corner of his eye he saw Tess reach into the garbage and retrieve the empty can. Without breaking stride, she placed it on the counter and followed him into the next room. He sat on the couch and waited as Tess seated herself on the chair facing him.

"All right, Ms. Phillips, why don't you give me some idea of your daily schedule, so I know what time to be here tomorrow."

"I beg your pardon?"

"You know, what time you get up in the morning, when you leave the house, that kind of schedule."

"Mr. Bartholomew, why would you possibly need that kind of information?" Tess was totally bewildered.

"First of all, Ms. Phillips, please call me Nick. The last person who called me Mr. Bartholomew was a very unpleasant English professor in college, and I prefer not to be reminded of him."

The same wicked grin that had melted her defenses earlier passed over his face, and Tess couldn't help responding. She smiled back at him and said, "As long as you call me Tess. I don't care much for formality, either."

"Okay, Tess, it's a deal." Surprising himself almost as much as her, Nick continued, "Why don't we get some dinner while we iron out the details for this interview?"

The quick surge of pleasure shocked and confused Tess. Trying to come up with a good reason to refuse, she grabbed the quickest one. "I'm not dressed to go out anywhere." She glanced down at the worn jeans and faded blue shirt. "But thanks for the invitation."

"Hey, do I look like I'm ready for the Pump Room?"

Tess looked at his sweat pants and running shoes, when a thought suddenly struck her. "Is that how you always dress when you're going out to interview someone?"

25

Nick smiled complacently. "No, I had these clothes in my car. I figured if I was going to be spending time with a runner, the least I could do was be prepared. When Donna told me you were out running, I just changed into this in my car, and voila."

"Well, that was convenient, wasn't it?" she said vaguely, her mind sorting out the implications of his last remark. "What exactly do you mean by 'spending time with a runner?' "

He looked impatient. "You won the marathon, that's why I'm here. I figure you probably run once in a while, and when you do, I'll run with you. It's good copy, the reporter trying to keep up with the jock." He didn't have to add *especially when the jock is a woman.*

"Now, wait a minute. I thought we were talking about an interview here. You know, you ask me questions, I answer them. Since when are we so chummy that we train together?"

Nick shot her an incredulous look. "Come on, Tess, you're a runner, right?" When Tess just looked at him, he continued, "What does a runner do? She runs, that's what she does. What are my readers going to want to know? They're going to want to know about how you run. How far you run, how fast you run, what you wear when you run, how you look when you run. That's why I'm going to run with you."

He'd leaned forward in his seat as he spoke, and the space between them seemed to have shrunk to nothing. Now he sank back onto the couch and said softly, "Does that answer your question?"

"One of them." She stared back at him, determined not to let him see how much his answer disturbed her.

The air in the room was heavy with the waves of energy pouring out of both of them. Then Nick stood, and the atmosphere lightened immediately.

"So let's get some Chinese food and discuss the rest of them. I never argue on an empty stomach."

In spite of herself, Tess felt her mouth curve. "It's hard to decline such a graciously worded invitation, but no thanks. I don't really want to go out tonight." The words *with you* were unspoken, but seemed to echo between them.

"Come on, Tess, we both have to eat. We also have some things to talk about. It's not going to kill you to have dinner with me, is it?"

Her lips quivered. "I'm not sure if it's fatal, but I suspect it could be dangerous." She watched him for a moment, then sighed. "I'll go put my shoes on and we can leave."

Her reluctance only confirmed his suspicions that she was hiding something, making him all the more determined to find out the truth. Nick was astonished by how much he'd cared about her answer. Tess had some angle here. He was certain of it. He had a week with her, and he was sure he would figure it out. Then why had he been unwilling to take 'no' for an answer?

It was her eyes, he decided. Her eyes didn't belong to a twenty-six-year-old hustler. They were too ... trusting, he thought. They didn't belong in a hustler's face. If a man stared into Tess Phillips's eyes long enough, he would begin to believe in all sorts of fairy tales.

Nick listed all the possible scams she could have going as he watched her leave the room. Unfortunately, they didn't distract him at all from the sight of her round bottom encased in snug, faded jeans.

\*\*\*

*Why did you agree to this?* Tess asked herself for at least the tenth time. The lights in the restaurant were intimately dim, and several fragrant, steaming Chinese dishes sat on the table between her and Nick. She looked down at her plate as she scooped up another shrimp. Nick Bartholomew was too attractive for his own good. And definitely too attractive for her own good, she admitted.

The sooner we get this over with, she told herself, the sooner he'll be gone and you can get on with your life. Tess didn't want to explore why that thought was so unappealing right now. She reminded herself again of the reason they were here, and firmly pushed out of her mind any traitorous thoughts about Nick himself.

"Well, Nick, when are you going to do this interview?"

He watched her as she spooned another serving of spicy chicken onto her plate. "I don't believe how much of this food you've eaten."

Swallowing another mouthful, she grinned. "I warned you to order more egg rolls." Her smile faded as Nick leaned back against the booth and gave her a calculating look.

"You know, you don't seem too happy about all of this."

Tess looked at him, astonished at his remark. "Of course, I'm not. Why would I be happy about telling a total stranger about myself so he can write about it for millions of other total strangers to read?"

With a cynical smile, he drawled, "Oh, I can think of one or two reasons."

"Such as?"

"Publicity, to begin with."

"Why would I want publicity?" She looked at him, puzzled.

"Come on, Tess. No one is that naive." He sighed. Talk about laying it on with a trowel. This babe definitely needed some acting lessons.

"I don't suppose that you've gotten any phone calls the last couple of days, have you?" His voice dripped sarcasm.

"What do you mean?" Tess looked so bewildered that for a moment, Nick almost believed she had no idea what he was talking about.

"Nobody's called to see if you'd be interested in becoming a spokesperson for their product?"

Tess stared at him for a moment. "Are you talking

about endorsements?" she finally asked.

"Yes, endorsements." He gave her a patronizing smile.

Tess smiled and leaned back against the booth. "Not a single call. I have an unlisted number," she said smugly. Her forehead creased. "Which reminds me. How did you get my number?"

"Your entry form." Nick was as smug as she had been. He leaned back and watched her. "So tell me, if you really don't want to be interviewed, why didn't you just refuse?"

"I couldn't. I signed the entry form." Tess's eyes flashed. "And don't think I didn't try to come up with a way."

"You could always just give back the money. Then you could send me on my merry way." He watched her carefully.

Tess avoided looking at him. "I can't do that." She missed the derisive gleam in his eyes. "I guess I'm stuck with you."

She swirled the straw around in her glass and finally looked at him. "You tell me when it's convenient for you and I'll give you your interview then."

"Tess, I don't think you understand. When you signed that entry form, and then won the race, you gave me permission to spend a week with you. I'm not interested in talking to you for two hours some afternoon. I'm going to spend the next week glued to you." He couldn't resist adding, "I want my readers to become very familiar with you."

Tess stared at him, horrified. "You're serious, aren't you?"

"Oh yes, I am."

"Nick, I can't bear the thought of having my whole life made public. I'm not one of your professional athletes, you know. There's nothing even remotely interesting about my life." She sounded like an idiot, she knew, but couldn't seem to stop.

If he was going to shadow her for the next week, she

thought despairingly, there was no way he wouldn't find out about the recycling center. And if he did, they might as well just close up shop right now.

There was no way she was going to let him expose their problems to the world. No one, she thought fiercely, would find out they were on the verge of bankruptcy. They'd find a way to keep the recycling center open, she assured herself. In the meantime, she'd let Nick Bartholomew know there were a few ground rules during the next week.

Tess took a deep breath. "All right, Nick, I guess I'm stuck with you. You can write anything you want about my running and my training, but I won't let you write about my personal life and especially not about my business."

"I'm glad we have that settled," Nick answered smoothly. He didn't bother to correct her. If she wanted to think that her personal life and her business were off limits that was fine with him. They weren't, of course, but he'd let her find that out later.

She was looking at him, and he couldn't quite meet her eyes. Now why should he feel guilty? He was just doing his job, getting the story any way he could. A little thing like a pair of trusting eyes had never bothered him before.

"Where do I meet you and when?"

"I guess you can meet me back at my house tomorrow afternoon at five. That's when I usually get home."

Nick had to stop himself from snorting in disgust. If this was an act for his benefit, it sure was wasted.

The waitress laid the check on the table, and as Nick searched through his wallet, he thought about the next week. It certainly was going to be interesting. They both stood up and walked toward the door. He watched the fluid, graceful sway of Tess's hips in her snug jeans.

Yes, a *most* interesting week.

# CHAPTER THREE

Tess propped her left leg on the back of a kitchen chair and bent over it. The muscles tightened, then stretched and lengthened. She stayed in that position for a few seconds, enjoying the sensation, then did the same for her right leg. Finally, she stood straight and walked to the kitchen door. Her hand was on the knob when she paused.

Should she really be doing this? After all, she had just run yesterday, and the marathon was only four days ago. Her legs were still a little stiff, she admitted. She hesitated for only a moment before opening the door. It didn't matter that her legs were still sore. Running always helped her to think more clearly and work out problems. And if she ever needed that help, she needed it today.

She started jogging down the drive, her feet automatically falling into a smooth rhythm. Turning into the street she felt, rather than saw, someone fall into step beside her. This time, she didn't stop. After a momentary falter, she just kept going. It didn't really surprise her. Nick Bartholomew wasn't going to be put off by anything so trivial as her desire for privacy.

" 'Morning, Tess," Nick said smoothly.

Tess just grunted. She had been telling the truth yesterday when she said she didn't like to talk while she was running. If he wanted to come with her she couldn't stop him, but he couldn't make her answer him.

Thirty minutes. Almost time to pick up the pace. Tess grinned to herself. She heard Nick's ragged breathing next to her, and knew he was tiring. She had to admit, he had been the perfect running partner so far. After the first good morning, he hadn't uttered a word. He adjusted his stride to hers, and they had fallen into an easy rhythm together.

Now, if only he had worn sweat pants instead of those skimpy nylon jogging shorts. Despite the fact that Tess was concentrating on running, she couldn't help noticing Nick's legs. Long and lean, the corded muscles were covered with fine black hairs. She watched, fascinated, as they gathered, then stretched with each stride. When she found herself wondering how those hard muscles would feel against her own legs, she blushed furiously and firmly turned her head away. She could only hope that Nick had been too preoccupied with keeping up with her to notice her staring.

Looking around, Tess realized that they were almost back to her house. *You were so busy ogling his legs*, she told herself disgustedly, *that you forgot your sprint*. She turned into her driveway and slowed down, and Nick stumbled to a halt beside her.

Once they were in her kitchen, Tess turned to Nick and said, "I thought we agreed that you'd meet me here at five o'clock this evening."

"No, we didn't," he answered between gasps. "You told me to be here then, but I never agreed." Still breathing hard, he watched her closely. "I told you, Tess, that I was going to spend the next week with you, and I meant it."

Tess stared at him for a moment, fuming. "Are you always so annoying, or are you making a special effort in my case?"

His lips twitched slightly, then curved into his cocky

grin. "Honey, show me a reporter who isn't annoying and I'll show you a reporter who's writing obituaries."

In spite of herself, an answering smile crept onto her face. She shook her head and turned away to do her post run stretching. As she bent over the chair again, she turned to Nick and said, "I take it you think you're coming to work with me today?"

"We can either drive together or I'll follow you there. Doesn't matter to me."

As she looked away again, she shrugged. "It's your gas." Nick didn't bother to answer her. He was too busy watching her stretch. He'd never seen Tess close up in running shorts before, and couldn't seem to take his eyes off her legs. They were long, sleek and firm, and they didn't stop until they got to her waist. She abruptly swung her leg off the chair, and Nick hastily looked away.

She was halfway to the bathroom when she stopped. Turning, she watched Nick lounge against the kitchen counter. Sweat dripped in little rivulets down his neck, plastering his shirt to his body. The wet material clung to his broad shoulders and outlined the muscles in his chest. "Um, if you'd like to take a shower, there's another bathroom in the basement. I suppose you can use it."

Pushing himself away from the counter, Nick gave her a lazy grin. "After a workout like we just had, I need to cool off." Running his fingers through his damp hair, he drawled, "You do know how to work up a sweat in a man."

Something fluttered in Tess's stomach as Nick held her eyes with his. She stared, mesmerized as his lazy grin disappeared, replaced by an intense, hungry look. His sweaty aroma, an acrid tang mixed with his woodsy aftershave, filled the room. When he took a step in her direction, the spell was broken. Tess said hurriedly, "There are towels and anything else you'll need under the sink." She turned and practically sprinted into her bathroom.

After her shower, Tess walked back into the kitchen to find Nick sitting at the table dressed in dark blue slacks and a striped shirt, reading her newspaper. The rich scent of freshly brewed coffee told her that he had made himself at home. Nick looked up from the paper and said, "How do you take your coffee?"

She probably should be annoyed, Tess thought, but a smile slipped onto her face. "It's nice to see that you know your way around a kitchen."

Nick gave her an answering grin as she sat down. "Which section do you want?" he asked, indicating the paper.

"Sports," she requested with a bland look.

"Here you go." He slid it across the table. "Nothing in it today, though."

Tess looked at him questioningly.

"My column doesn't run today," he explained.

She chuckled and leaned back with her coffee as she looked over the first page. "There's something very refreshing about a modest man."

Half an hour later, Tess glanced at the clock then reluctantly stood up and carried her cup to the sink. She had to admit, she'd almost enjoyed having breakfast with him. They'd read the paper and drank their coffee in a companionable silence, talking only rarely. Thank goodness, he wasn't a morning babbler.

Running and breakfast were one thing, but her job was something else again. She stood at the counter chewing on the inside of her cheek, thinking. There was no way she could stop him from following her to work. What she needed was a diversion.

"Excuse me for a moment, Nick," she said sweetly. Walking through the kitchen door, she turned into the bathroom. Closing the door, she let the water run for a minute, then opened the door a crack and peeked out. He was engrossed in the newspaper again, not even glancing her way. She turned off the water, dashed into the living room, grabbed her purse and keys and was out the door before Nick even realized she was gone.

The car was at the end of the driveway, turning into the street, when Nick burst through the front door. "What the hell do you think you're doing?" he shouted furiously.

"I'll see you at five o'clock." She waved gaily from the open window of her car before she pressed the accelerator and sped off.

\*\*\*

The bang of the office door slamming shut made Tess jump in her chair. She looked up into Nick's face, only inches from hers.

"Cute, Ms. Phillips, real cute," he murmured into her ear. His blue eyes were almost black, and his brows were drawn together into a straight line above them. "We need to have a little talk." Without giving her a chance to answer, he grabbed her wrist and pulled her out of her chair.

They were flying out the door before Tess could open her mouth. "Okay," he said, once they were outside, "what exactly was that little game all about?"

Tess glanced at her watch. "I am impressed, Bartholomew. Only an hour to find me. Your sources must be pretty good."

"Cut the crap, Tess. What the hell were you trying to do? I told you I was going to go to work with you today."

"And I told you that my personal life was off limits! I meant it, Nick. You have no right to follow me here and nose around my business."

"Oh, so you own this business, do you? What is this place, anyway?"

Mentally kicking herself for handing him that bit of information, Tess ground out, "Just leave, will you?" The blood was pounding behind her eyes and swirling around in her head. She didn't want to give him the satisfaction of seeing how upset she was that he had tracked her down so easily.

"After all the trouble it took to find you? Not a chance, honey." Tess tried to walk around him, but he reached out and put his hands on her shoulders, holding her in front of him. "From now on, you and I are joined at the hip."

Tess reached up to free herself. Curling her fingers around the insides of his wrists, she started to push his hands away, then suddenly stopped. His palms gripped her shoulders a little more tightly, then abruptly loosened and slid down to her upper arms. Her anger mingled with a wisp of desire. The hands that had held her so rigidly just a moment ago were now gently massaging her muscles, caressing the soft skin on the inside of her arm. Ten different sensations shimmered through her nerves and swirled around her insides, none of them even remotely related to the anger she had been feeling.

Shocked at the way her body was betraying her, she looked up at Nick. That was a big mistake, she realized as soon as her eyes met his. Their dark blue depths glittered with an emotion that she had no trouble identifying, because it was the same unexpected desire she felt. Muttering something under her breath, she pulled away from him and started back into the building.

"What did you say, Tess?" He watched her hasty retreat with a bemused look.

"I said you were a pain in the butt, Bartholomew." The door banged shut behind her.

When Nick walked back into the office a few minutes later, she didn't even bother to look up. There was no way short of dynamite she would dislodge him from her office now, she knew. Out of the corner of her eye she watched him saunter over to the window. Her eyes followed his line of sight as he shoved his hands into his pockets, staring at the commotion outside.

Several cars were lined up at the row of receptacles

opposite the office building. Men and women were busily emptying bags and boxes of bottles and cans into the large bins. The almost constant sound of glass breaking was only the background noise. Heavy trucks rumbled in and out of the asphalt-paved yard, dumping their loads of more cans and bottles into other dumpsters. Tess saw the familiar sights with one glance and looked back at Nick. He seemed to be fascinated with all he saw.

"Hey, Tess!" She turned around at the sound of her partner's voice. "It's your turn this week to go watch them weigh the stuff. Steve is just about ready to leave."

"I'm on my way, Mike." She turned off her calculator and pushed away from her desk. Nick fell into step beside her as she walked out the door. Ignoring him, she walked to her car, opened it and slid in. By the time she had put on her seat belt and started the engine, he was sitting next to her.

"Where do you think you're going, Bartholomew?" she scowled at him.

"I have no idea, Tess. Why don't you tell me?"

Fuming, she gunned the motor a few times while they sat there. Finally she turned to him and said, "Look, Nick, I don't want you here. Why can't you just be a gentleman and meet me back at my house tonight at five o'clock?"

He raised his eyebrows. "First of all, honey, I've been called a lot of names, but nobody has ever accused me of being a gentleman. If you're counting on any chivalrous feelings from me, you're out of luck. Second, if I get out of this car, it's going to be with one hell of a scene. If you want everybody who works for you to see the fireworks, I'll be happy to oblige you. If not, I suggest you put this car in gear."

Furious, she just glared at him. It made her even angrier to realize how accurately he had her pegged. The last thing she wanted was a scene at her office, and he knew it. Admitting defeat for now, she slammed the car into gear and roared out of the yard.

Nick leaned his arm across the back of the passenger seat and turned so he was facing Tess. He smiled to himself as he thought of that last look she'd given him. If looks could kill, he'd be six feet under pushing up daisies. Right now, she was concentrating on traffic, so Nick was free to study her.

She looked ... stunning, he admitted. Her high cheekbones gave her face a look of elegance, and the determined chin gave it character. The khaki pants and floral patterned sweater in different hues of rose flattered her slender frame and emphasized the shades of gold in her hair. He almost reached out and lifted the heavy braid, he was so fascinated by the intermingling of colors. Another woman could have spent hours in a beauty salon and still not come close to duplicating it. Every shade of blond was woven through it, from the palest white to deep, deep gold.

And that braid. Why did a woman with such glorious hair insist on binding it to her head like that? Soon, he promised himself, he would watch her hair swinging free. The thought of Tess standing in front of him with her hair unbound made him move restlessly in his seat. It also reminded him of why he was here with her. Almost reluctantly, he took out his tape recorder. Even as he turned to face her, he reminded himself to keep his distance.

Out of the corner of her eye Tess saw him lay the tape recorder on his lap. She heard the click as he turned it on and took a deep breath.

"So tell me about your recycling center, Tess."

"I'm surprised that you recognized what it was." Even to herself, Tess sounded childish.

"Hey, I watch public television sometimes, too," he answered breezily. He wiggled his eyebrows and gave his best Groucho Marx leer. "Some of the programs are quite educational, know what I mean?"

In spite of herself, Tess had to laugh. She knew she

would be better off if she just stayed angry at him, but she was afraid that was going to be impossible. He was just too charming to be unleashed without a written warning.

"At least tell me where we're going right now."

Tess sighed with exasperation. "You really don't give up, do you?"

"Look, I'll find out where we're going as soon as we get there. You're not going to be giving away any state secrets by telling me a few minutes early," he said reasonably.

She stared out the windshield, but her knuckles whitened on the steering wheel. For a long moment she watched blindly out the window as the small, tidy homes lining the tree-shaded streets flashed past. Finally she sighed.

"We're going to the company that buys some of the material we collect. We have to watch as they weigh the stuff to make sure they don't cheat us."

Shaking his head sadly, he said, "Such a suspicious mind."

"It's a practice that protects both us and the buyer," she replied primly. "It's standard procedure for recycling companies."

As she spoke they turned into an asphalt-paved yard that looked very much like the one they had just left. One of their trucks with the name Greener Earth and their emblem of a tree painted on it stood in the yard in front of them. Tess pulled over to the side, stopped with a jerk, and jumped out.

Without waiting for Nick, she strode through the door of the closest building into a scene of what appeared to be total chaos. The level of sound was deafening. The noise of glass breaking, cans being crushed, and newspaper being shredded blended into an almost unbearable din.

Tess casually picked up a yellow hard hat as a man wearing an identical hat hurried toward her. At the sight of his familiar long ponytail, diamond earring, and faded jeans her face lit up.

"Will!  It's good to see you again."

"Likewise, Tess.  Hey, congratulations on the race last week.  When I saw you on the news, it really freaked me out."  He hooked an arm over her shoulder as they walked along.  "Though why anyone would want to work that hard is a mystery to me."

Tess's laugh gurgled in her throat.  "Thanks, Will.  I think."

"Who's the slick-looking dude?"  Will nodded in Nick's direction.

"Nick Bartholomew, Will Mahoney," Tess answered tersely.  The two men shook hands, and Will watched her expectantly.  Tess sighed.  "Nick is a reporter for the Chicago Post."  She turned to Nick and explained, "Will owns the company that processes our raw material and finds users for it."

As she finished speaking, they reached a large door open to the outside.  The truck from the Greener Earth had backed into the building and positioned itself in front of a huge revolving drum.  Slowly the back of the dump truck lifted, until a shiny stream of aluminum cans rattled and crashed into the mouth of the drum.  Tess watched numbers flash on a digital readout until one number glowed steadily.  She nodded to Will, and jotted the number down on a piece of paper.

"What's going on?"  Nick's breath tickled her neck, and his hand brushed the hairs on her arm.  The echoing noise near the machines was so loud that it was impossible to hear unless the words were spoken directly into her ear.  Nick's body brushed hers again as he moved closer to hear her answer.

The heat from his body radiated into hers, making her temperature rise several degrees.  The hard muscles and lean lines of his frame were temptingly close, and she clutched the paper and pencil more tightly to prevent her hands from reaching out to touch him.  When he bent his head to hear her answer, his hair tickled her nose and the scent of his aftershave, woodsy and male, filled her head. Licking her lips nervously, she took a step away from him.

"I couldn't hear you," he shouted into her ear.

She had to get out of the noisy, deafening barn. If she had to stand this close to Nick for another second, she would do something that she knew she'd regret. As she walked quickly toward the open door the sound level dropped suddenly, even though her ears were still ringing.

Standing with a safe distance between her and Nick, she asked, "Now, what were you saying?"

"I just wanted to know what they were doing."

"That machine was weighing the cans. I was making a note of the amount so we could double check it when we get Will's statement." Tess was fervently grateful that Nick hadn't seemed to notice her reaction back in the building. She'd give him just about any information he wanted right now if it kept his attention off her and on her business.

As they drove back to the Greener Earth, neither of them spoke. Tess snuck a glance at Nick now and then, remembering the way his body felt standing close to hers. Just thinking about it made her tingle again. Yes, it was going to be a very long week.

Nick broke the silence, saying suddenly, "This explains the soda can yesterday."

She looked at him, puzzled, and he grinned. "I threw my empty cola can into your garbage yesterday. You just pulled it right back out and set it on the counter. I don't think you even realized what you were doing."

"Probably not." Smiling back at him, she added, "At least I didn't give you the ten minute lecture about conserving natural resources. You should be grateful I was thinking about something else."

The rest of the day passed quickly. Tess tried, unsuccessfully, to ignore Nick and concentrate on her paperwork. Even though he asked very few questions, apparently content for now to sit in a chair and watch, she was acutely aware of his presence. She knew at any given moment where he was in the room. When he had walked over to her desk once or twice to look at something, the air had vibrated between them. Looking up to see that it was almost time to leave, she sighed with relief. She'd spent more than enough time with Nick Bartholomew today.

Gathering up her purse and keys, she said brightly, "That's about it for today. Ready to go?"

Nick uncurled his lean body from the depths of the easy chair and stood up. "Anytime you are."

Her Japanese economy car and Nick's sleek sports model were the only two cars left in the yard. Tess opened the door, then paused before getting in. "I suppose you plan on being here tomorrow?"

"You can count on it, honey."

The cocky grin made her grind her teeth. Slamming the car door, she roared out of the yard. At least, she thought, she would have the evening to regain her balance. She wasn't sure if the thought of spending the next week with Nick was thrilling or terrifying to her. The problem was, she was afraid it was both.

Immersed in her thoughts, she pulled into her driveway and got out of the car before she realized that Nick had followed her home. When she saw him leaning against his car, she stopped dead and stared at him. "What are you doing here?"

"I thought we had a date for five o'clock. I'm a few minutes early, but chalk it up to eagerness."

"You spent the whole day trailing after me," she began furiously, "and now you expect me to spend the evening with you, too?" She wanted to shove him back into his car and run into the house. The last thing she needed right now was to spend more time with Nick. She had spent too much time with him already today, and she was too tired to put up the fences that were necessary to protect her business.

As she stared defiantly at him, his face suddenly

softened, losing the arrogant cockiness that was usually present. A look of understanding flashed in his eyes as his lips curved into a genuine smile. "Don't worry, Tess, I won't badger you unmercifully tonight. We'll order a pizza and just talk, okay?"

Tess looked into Nick's eyes, and the sympathy she saw there made her soften inside. For a moment, her heart fluttered, but she pushed the feeling away ruthlessly. There was no way she wanted to like Nick Bartholomew.

Nick tried to keep his face expressionless as he followed Tess into the house. *If you get involved with her*, he reminded himself grimly, *this story is shot to hell*. He was appalled at how quickly she had gotten around his defenses. He told himself again that no one can win a marathon the first time they run one. She had to be pulling a scam, he assured himself, but she sure did seem like a genuine innocent. In no way did she resemble the jaded, arrogant athletes he was used to interviewing.

It was that recycling center today, he knew. She and Mike and Donna were so sincere and so convinced that what they were doing was vital. Hell, he guessed it was, but he'd never thought much about where he put his garbage. He suspected, though, that by the end of the week he wouldn't be able to toss a soda can into the garbage without serious guilt.

Tess excused herself and Nick went to the phone to order a pizza. By the time she returned, Nick was seated on the couch with his tape recorder perched on the cushion next to him. Tess looked at it, and sat down on the couch at the opposite end.

"I ordered a pizza. Pepperoni and mushrooms, is that okay?"

"And extra cheese, I hope?" Tess said lightly.

Nick raised his eyebrows. "That goes without saying."

She smiled and relaxed a little. Not too much, though. That could prove to be a fatal mistake.

"Tell me about the recycling center, Tess."

She looked at him, startled. She had expected a totally different question. Nick smiled in response.

"We'll get to the running, don't worry. I like to find out what makes people tick, and the recycling center is obviously important to you."

"Yes, it is," she said slowly, "and that's why I told you I don't want it to be part of your article. I'd rather not talk about the Greener Earth at all."

His eyebrows soared in disbelief. "You're turning down free publicity? You know how many people will read this article? The day after my column runs, your phone will be ringing off the wall."

"We don't need the publicity," she insisted.

Narrowing his eyes, Nick stared at her. "Businesses usually need all the publicity they can get. When it's free, that's even better. Why doesn't the Greener Earth need publicity, Tess?"

"We just don't." Realizing she was practically shouting, Tess lowered her voice. "There's no reason you need to write anything about the Greener Earth. Just leave it out of your story."

Nick leaned back on the couch. "I think it might be more fun to find out why you don't want me to know anything about your company." He saw the panic jump into her eyes, and almost smiled. She was almost too easy to read. *Now what kind of hanky panky is going on at the recycling center, and what does it have to do with the marathon?* This was what he had expected. He could almost smell the dirt she was trying to hide.

"Listen, Tess," he started smoothly, "you might as well tell me something about the Greener Earth. I can find out most of what I want to know anyway, and you could at least make sure I have it right."

Licking her lips, Tess stared at his tape recorder for a few moments. He was suspicious already, that was pretty obvious. Maybe she should answer a few little questions, she thought, to keep him from asking the big ones. "All right," she said in a low voice, not looking at him, "what do you want to know?"

"How long has it been open?"

She looked up in surprise. She hadn't expected him to ask such an innocuous question. "Just over two years."

"And you own the place?"

"Mike Borgren and I are partners in the business."

"Why did you decide to start a recycling center?"

For the first time since she'd sat down, Tess relaxed slightly and smiled at him. "You don't want to hear my half-hour rap on landfills, the environment, and being good stewards of the land. Let's just say I am extremely concerned about the environment, and recycling was one way that I felt I could contribute and make a difference."

"Who is Mike and how did you become partners?" He stared down at his notebook as he scribbled some meaningless shorthand symbols. He had no more interest in this question than the others he'd asked, he assured himself.

Tess seemed to find nothing odd about the question. "Mike Borgren and I met three years ago, working for the same company. We were both interested in recycling, and when I decided to quit and open the Greener Earth, he came along as my partner."

Nick closed his notebook and looked at her. "You want me to believe that you sit around on dates and discuss recycling?"

Her eyes challenged him. "First of all, I never said Mike and I were dating. And second, recycling was an issue that we had to deal with almost daily in our previous jobs."

"Okay, what was your previous job?"

Her hesitation was momentary. "We worked for a company that made plastic and Styrofoam containers for food. The kind that aren't biodegradable. The kind that are buried in landfills and will still be here hundreds of years from now."

"If you felt that way, why were you working for the company in the first place?"

Her eyes flashed at him. "You never had to work for a company or at a job you disliked?"

"You can always quit a job, you know."

"Which is exactly what I did."

Nick filed the note away in the back of his mind. *Find out where she used to work.* She might as well have waved a red flag at him. Her open book of a face was making his job a lot easier.

He asked her a few more questions about the day-to-day running of the center, and she told him how they made their money by selling what they collected to various companies that reused the materials. By the time the doorbell rang, Nick had a fairly comprehensive idea of how the recycling center worked.

Tess looked up, startled. She had been concentrating so hard on what she could safely tell Nick and what she had to avoid that she had forgotten all about their dinner. Nick turned off the tape recorder and stood up. "I'll get it, it's probably the pizza."

With a sigh of relief she watched him open the door, then went into the kitchen. When she returned with plates, glasses, and two bottles of soda, Nick had opened the pizza box and set it on the tale. The aroma of tomato sauce, herbs, and melted cheese filled the air, and Tess realized that she was ravenous.

"I never could resist pizza," she admitted as she sat down, letting some of the tension seep out of her bones.

"That's the first chink in the armor." Nick's voice was completely serious.

When Tess gave him a quizzical look, he explained. "When I find out what a person's weaknesses are, I take full advantage of them. I figure that from now on, if I show up at your door with a pizza, you'll be like melted mozzarella in my hands."

Tess smiled. "In your dreams, Bartholomew." She

took another bite and closed her eyes. "Although I will admit, it would be a close call."

While they were eating, Nick asked about her family. She paused, then told him that she was an only child. She explained that her parents had died when she was very young, and she'd been raised by her uncle. She changed the subject by asking him about his family. For the rest of the meal, he entertained her with stories about his two brothers and two sisters and their youthful escapades.

When the pizza was finished, they both leaned back, content and relaxed. Finally, Tess asked lazily, "Don't you want to talk about my running?"

"Later." Nick leaned forward. "Right now there's something much more important I need to ask you."

In spite of everything he'd been telling himself for the last hour, he reached out his hand and captured her braid. At that moment, he knew exactly how a moth felt when confronted with a flame. "Why do you pull your hair back like this?"

Tess's gaze flew from his hand to his face. Suddenly she didn't feel relaxed anymore. She sat up slowly, her heartbeat so loud in her ears that she was certain Nick could hear it, too. "Ah, I always braid it when I'm working." Even to herself, her voice sounded weak.

"You're not working now, are you?" Nick's voice was low and gravelly. Tess avoided his eyes. She was afraid she knew what she would see there.

"This interview is work."

"My tape recorder is off. No notebook in sight. We're on our own time now, Tess."

"Well, then, I guess it's time I ..." Tess started to rise, but Nick's hold on her braid stopped her. Slowly, she sat back down. When she finally looked at him, his eyes caught and held hers. What she saw there made her pulse pound.

Without taking his eyes off hers, Nick slid his hand lightly down the length of her braid. The slight tug on her scalp sent a wisp of desire curling through her.

His hand found the band that held the braid together. His fingers fumbled for a moment, then she felt the band pull free. He slowly brought his other hand to her head, and with both hands teased her hair out of the braid. His dark blue eyes seemed to turn almost black as he watched her hair tumble around her face. Every time his fingers brushed her scalp, she felt the tingle in the pit of her stomach. She had never in her life known that hair could be so ... stimulating.

Finally her hair hung in heavy waves over her shoulders and brushed the tops of her breasts. When Nick slowly took his hands away, Tess saw they were trembling. She could feel herself trembling, too, and her heart pounded faster every moment.

"I've imagined you like this since the first time I saw you, at the race," Nick murmured. He put up a shaking hand and ran his fingers through her hair again, then cupped the back of her neck and drew her toward him.

Tess acknowledged vaguely that she should stop, but desire was pulsing through her blood and her lips tingled with anticipation. If she was truthful, she would admit that this was what she'd wanted all day. She'd never imagined Nick's hands could be this gentle. The fingers on her neck softly massaged, while his other palm traced slow circles on her back. When their noses were almost touching, Nick brought both hands up to cup her face.

The first touch of his lips was so slight, it was as if a breeze had kissed her. He rubbed his thumb softly over her lower lip, and followed it with his mouth. Tess felt as if she'd swallowed fireworks that sizzled and popped in her stomach. Her lips burned where Nick's had touched them. When he took his mouth away, she licked her lips as if to savor his taste.

Nick groaned and found her mouth once again. This time, he took her greedily, as if he couldn't get enough of her. His teeth nipped gently at her lower lip, until she opened her mouth to cry out with the pleasure. His tongue slipped inside, caressing and stroking until Tess was aware of nothing except Nick.

She was pressed against Nick as if their bodies were fused. Tess didn't remember moving, but his legs held her in a vise grip. Nick's hands were roaming up and down her back, lighting fires wherever they touched. His fingers lazily circled closer and closer to the side of her breast, never quite reaching it but turning her insides to jelly.

Finally Nick moved his lips from her mouth. They roamed over her face, touching and tasting every inch of her. His hands moved up, and tangled in her hair as he cupped the back of her head and tried to draw her even closer.

"Tess," Nick murmured, almost as if to himself. "Tess."

He slipped his hand beneath her sweater and stroked the sensitive skin of her stomach. It was as if he'd dipped his hand in fire, and was trailing flames wherever he touched. As his hand crept higher and higher, Tess turned and found his mouth. This time, it was she that took greedily, driving them both to the edge of sanity.

The shrill ringing of the telephone made both Tess and Nick freeze. Nick raised his head and stared at her. Neither of them moved a muscle as they listened to the insistent sound. When it finally stopped, Tess exhaled shakily. She hadn't realized she had been holding her breath.

Tess looked down at her bare abdomen. At some point her sweater had crept up around her chest. Without looking at Nick, she reached up with a shaking hand and pulled it down. When she swung her legs off the couch and tried to stand up, Nick took both her hands and held her there.

"Tess."

She looked down at their joined hands. God help her, even the slight pressure of his fingers curled around hers was enough to make her melt.

"Tess, I'm not sorry, and I hope you aren't either."

She raised her head then and looked at him steadily. "Is this what's known as objective journalism, Nick?" She reddened slightly and turned away. "Getting the story no matter what the cost?"

"You can't believe this had anything to do with my interviewing you?" Nick sounded genuinely astonished. "My God, Tess, what kind of person do you think I am?"

Tess gently disengaged her hands. "I don't know. I thought maybe I was beginning to figure it out, but I'm not so sure anymore."

Tess touched her lips. They were swollen and soft and incredibly sensitive. Remembering the exact taste of Nick's mouth on hers, she trembled again and stood up.

"Good night, Nick. I'll see you in the morning."

She felt him come up behind her, and expected some glib remark. Instead, his hand stroked her hair one more rime, and his breath whispered in her ear. "Until tomorrow, Tess."

She stood there a moment longer, and heard the soft click of the door closing. Walking back to the couch, she dropped down into its softness, wanting only to be nestled and comforted. Instead, Nick's masculine scent surrounded her, wafting up from the cushions. She hesitated only a moment before burrowing her face into the cushions, drinking in his smell.

Nick paused outside the door, not wanting to leave. Finally he walked to his car and got inside. He sat staring out the windshield, making no move to start the car.

God, how could he have been so stupid? His brains had relocated below his waist. He thought of Tess again, lying on the couch with her hair tangled around her face and her sweater sliding up her belly, and he shifted uncomfortably. His brain was overly active tonight.

The worst part was, he really had forgotten all about the interview. It was Tess who had filled his entire mind, driven away all thoughts other than desire for her. It wasn't what he was used to. He didn't like caring about someone he was supposed to interview. It could throw off his timing, take the edge off. It would ruin his column, damn it.

Nick tried to recall the hostility he'd felt for Tess Phillips. If he was going to succeed in discovering her angle, he needed to get that back. He told himself firmly that was just what he intended to do. Feeling her moan against his lips again, he turned the ignition key with a savage jerk. He cursed steadily and vividly all the way home.

# CHAPTER FOUR

Tess unlocked the door of the office and walked in. She smiled to herself as she glanced at the clock. Nick would be standing at her door right about now, she figured, wondering why she didn't answer his knock. Her smile widened as she imagined his reaction. Nick Bartholomew was a man who didn't like being outwitted. Relishing that thought, she sat down at her desk and turned happily to her work.

Half an hour later, Tess looked up from the paper she was studying to see a man standing in the doorway. She gave a startled shriek and instinctively flinched away from him.

"Nick!" She drew in a deep, shaky breath. "Was it absolutely necessary to sneak up on me like that?"

"I just walked in the door," he pointed out. "It's not my fault that you find garbage so engrossing."

Tess glanced down at the paper she'd been reading, and deliberately pushed it under a stack of files. When she looked up, Nick was staring at her speculatively, but as his eyes met hers his expression changed. Suddenly, their eyes locked and the air hummed with memories of desire. Then Tess looked away, and the moment vanished.

"You about ready for breakfast?" Nick held up a familiar orange and pink bag and flashed his crooked grin.

"I got donuts."

"How do you know I haven't already eaten breakfast?" Tess demanded, disturbed by her immediate reaction to Nick. Wasn't it only last night that she'd convinced herself he was only trying to get a better story and she wasn't interested in him anyway?

"Hey, no problem. I'll eat them myself."

Tess watched Nick remove a donut from the bag and take a bite. Smiling in spite of herself, she jumped up and grabbed the bag from him.

"You're a jerk, Bartholomew," she said between mouthfuls of a cream-filled bismark.

Nick passed her a large cup of coffee. "Tess, you're going to have to stop showering me with these effusive thank-yous. It's getting embarrassing."

Tess grinned and sipped her coffee, completely at ease again.

"Ah, Tess," he began slowly, "about last night ..."

The smile disappeared from her face as if wiped away with an eraser. She hadn't moved, but Nick could feel the distance that was suddenly between them.

"You were right, I was out of line," he murmured. "It shouldn't have happened, and it won't happen again."

She watched him steadily. "Strictly business from now on, Nick?"

"If that's what you want, Tess, that's what it is."

Tess's gaze flickered over him and dropped back to her desk. Finally she said in a low voice, "It's what I want."

It appalled her to realize that it was exactly the opposite of what she wanted. If she told Nick the truth, she would say she wanted nothing more than a repeat of the previous evening. She stared blindly at the papers jumbled over the desk. There was no way Nick Bartholomew was going to find out how she felt. She would keep it impersonal, keep it business, and keep away from him.

She heard Nick moving around behind her. Tess couldn't stop herself from peeking over her shoulder. He was looking through some magazines that Donna kept in a rack next to her desk. With a feeling of relief, Tess saw him pick up a copy of a news magazine and fold himself into a chair. She removed the paper she'd slid away from Nick's view and picked up her calculator.

She barely glanced up when Mike and Donna arrived at the office. Now, several hours later, she looked up with a start as Mike plopped himself on the corner of her desk.

"So, Tess." He picked up the papers she was working on and glanced at them. "Are we going to be here next month, or what?"

Tess couldn't believe her ears. Equal parts of fear and anger blazed out of her eyes at him. "Yes, Mike," she forced out through clenched teeth, "we are most definitely going to be here next month." Tess's eyes moved in Nick's direction, then back to Mike. "Perhaps we could continue this conversation some other time."

Mike stared at Tess for a moment, puzzled. Tess stared back with narrowed eyes, then gave a quick jerk of her head in Nick's direction. Mike glanced over at Nick, then suddenly realized what Tess was trying to say.

Leaning close to Tess, he stage whispered, "Sorry, I wasn't thinking."

Tess fumed. She stood up and stalked to the door, then turned and said to her partner in a deceptively mild voice, "Mike, there's something I've been meaning to ask you about the collection bins. Do you have a minute now to take a look at them?"

As soon as Mike stood up, Tess was out the door. By the time Mike caught up with her, she was half way across the yard. "Hey, Tess, what's eating you today?"

She whirled on him. "Where exactly did you leave your mind this morning? That reporter in there is salivating right now over those juicy little tidbits you just fed him."

Tess ran her fingers over her hair, loosening a few strands of her braid. "Do you want all the suburbs around here to find out that we're on the brink of collapse?" She stared at Mike angrily until he looked away, uncomfortable.

"I think you're getting a little paranoid, Tess. What difference does it make if the guy finds out that the Greener Earth is in trouble? He's writing about you winning the marathon, not this recycling center."

"He's writing about me, Mike. Do you seriously think that a little item like the fact that the Greener Earth is in trouble and only the money I won in the marathon saved it from closing isn't going to be interesting to him? If he found that out, we'd be the headlines in his column the next day."

"I thought we agreed that we needed more publicity."

"Don't be an idiot," Tess answered hotly. "How many suburbs are we negotiating with right now, five?" When Mike nodded, Tess continued, "Do you think that if they found out we were in trouble they'd sign a contract with us?"

Without waiting for Mike to answer, Tess rounded on him. "Of course, they wouldn't. They'd run, not walk, in any other direction but to us. And if the Greener Earth is going to make it, we have to have those new routes."

They walked a few steps in silence, then Mike draped an arm over Tess's shoulders. "You're right, partner. I screwed up. From now on, my lips are sealed. Bartholomew can torture me, he can get out the cattle prod, he can dangle donuts under my nose, but I won't squeal."

Tess's anger melted away. "If I see any jelly stains on your face, buster, you're going to have to do some pretty fast talking," she warned with a smile.

From where he sat, Nick could see almost the whole yard. He'd been watching Mike and Tess while pretending to be reading the magazine. They were obviously having a fight, and it didn't take a genius to figure out that it had something to do with Mike's remark about the center still being here next month.

Nick watched Tess's hands knife through the air as she

spoke, then comb wildly through her hair. He grinned to himself as her neat braid became just the slightest bit tousled. Beneath that veneer of control, the lady had quite a temper.

His face still in the magazine, Nick continued to observe Tess and Mike. Then, as suddenly as it had started, the fight seemed to be over. Tess was laughing and Mike had his hands all over her. Every muscle in Nick's body immediately clenched into a giant fist, poised to strike. He was halfway out of his chair when he caught himself and slowly sat back down.

*What's your problem, Bartholomew?* Nick was puzzled and vaguely uneasy. This was a woman he was interviewing, nothing more. He pushed images of the previous evening firmly out of his mind. He didn't think he wanted to analyze his reaction just now. He'd be smarter to pay attention to what he was here for and try to figure out what Tess and Mike were talking about.

Nick glanced out the window one more time as Mike and Tess strolled in the direction of the collection bins, apparently in complete harmony. A few subtle questions to Tess, he decided, and he'd have the beginning of the solution. She'd needed the money she won too badly. He'd known it the instant he asked her why she hadn't given the money back if she was so dead set against the interview. Money was a powerful motivator. It could drive people to do unthinkable things. Nick's mouth tightened. He knew that better than most. And the amount of money floating around the sports world could tempt even a saint.

Nick turned back to his magazine. Tess and Mike had disappeared from view, hidden by the large open collection bins. He was content to bide his time. As soon as he got Tess alone, though, he would find out what was going wrong with the Greener Earth recycling center.

\*\*\*

"Honestly, Nick, I'm just going to the bank." Tess ran her hand over her hair in exasperation. When he'd said joined at the hip yesterday, he'd meant it literally. "Are you really going to insist on coming with me?"

As she glared at him across the top of her car, he shrugged and got in. "I don't have anything better to do," he pointed out.

Her car was too small, she realized suddenly as they drove through Oak Ridge. After last night she was too aware of him, and the close confines of her compact car brought his leg disturbingly close to hers. His hand rested only inches away from her thigh, and out of the corner of her eye she watched his chest rise and fall with every breath. She rolled the window down a shade farther. All of a sudden the car seemed too stuffy.

She breathed a sigh of relief as they pulled into the bank's parking lot. Before she could ask him if he intended to watch her transactions inside, a beeping noise filled the car. It took her a second to remember the small beeper he carried on his belt. Without even looking at it, he turned it off. Getting out of the car, he watched her get out and lock her door.

When she couldn't stand it for another second, she burst out, "Aren't you even going to look at it?"

He shook his head. "Nothing there to see. It just means I'm supposed to call the office."

As they entered the bank, Nick headed toward the public phones while she walked up to one of the tellers. He was still on the phone when she walked back into the lobby. Not wanting to seem as though she was eavesdropping, she examined a rack of pamphlets while he talked in a low voice into the phone.

When he finally hung up, his eyes were sparkling and he hurried over to her. "Do you have to get right back to the office?"

She shook her head. "No, but ..."

"Great. I've got a story that I need to cover right away, and I'd really rather not go all the way back to the Greener Earth to pick up my car. Do you mind coming with me?"

"I guess not," she said faintly. In spite of her determination to keep her distance from him, the thought of watching him at work was almost irresistible. She would merely be checking out his methods to know what she could expect, she assured herself.

When he told her they were headed out to the stadium in the far western suburbs where the professional football team played, she raised her eyebrows and headed the car in that direction. Nick didn't say a word during the trip. Every time she looked at him, he was staring out the window or scribbling in the notebook he carried in his back pocket. He was so charged up, Tess was sure that if she touched him she would get a shock.

"Are you always this excited about your work?"

Grinning at her, he ran his fingers through his hair. "According to my editor, nobody else knows about this story. One of the oldest guys on the team supposedly just quit. He's been with the team forever. The grand old man of the Chicago Warriors. If it's true, and if nobody else knows about it, it'll be the scoop of the week. Hell, maybe even of the month."

As they neared the stadium, Nick directed her to a parking spot near a number of other cars. "Those are the players' cars," he explained. "Jack's car is still over there, so we know he hasn't left yet. We'll wait in the car until we see him." He misinterpreted her questioning look. "We don't want any of the football beat reporters to see us. They'd wonder why we we're here."

"You actually know all the football players' cars by sight?" She wasn't sure whether to believe him or not.

He shrugged. "It's my job to know those things. You never know when you might need a little piece of information like that."

They waited in silence as Nick scanned over the

parking lot. Suddenly he jumped out of the car, pulling her with him. "There he is!"

Walking slowly toward them was a huge man. A man, she thought to herself, who wouldn't have been out of place in a Mr. Universe contest. His enormous shoulders strained at the material of his polo shirt. His thighs, encased in blue jeans, were the biggest she'd ever seen. As she watched him get closer, she noticed the limp. The pain on his face each time his left leg moved forward was obvious.

"Hey, Jack," Nick said softly.

The man looked over at them, and a tired smile crossed his face. "Hey yourself, Bartholomew. What are you doing out here?"

"Someone told me that the greatest offensive lineman that ever played the game had just retired, and I came to find out for myself."

Jack gave a snort. "Retired, huh. Is that what they call it?"

"What do you mean?"

The tall man slumped back on the fender of his car. "They dumped me, Nick. Told me I was too old to fit in with their 'youth movement.' Just like that, without any warning. You know I'd planned to retire at the end of this season anyway," he added bitterly. "I guess that wasn't soon enough for them."

For the next half hour Tess watched, fascinated and incredibly moved, as Nick talked quietly to the man, sympathizing without ever patronizing him. When Jack Abbott finally got into his car, Nick leaned in the window to shake his hand one last time. "If there's anything I can do for you, Jack, you let me know."

As he started his car, the other man nodded. "Yeah, Nick, I will. Nobody else would have cared enough to come out here right away like this. I appreciate it."

Nick stood next to her as they watched the car drive away. "Sons of bitches," he swore viciously under his breath. "Come on, let's get out of here."

They were half way back to the Greener Earth before either of them spoke. Nick's glowering frown was the complete opposite of his excitement on the drive out to the football stadium. Suddenly he swore under his breath again and turned to her. "That man is one of the most decent men involved in professional sports. One of the few," he added. "He had this last year left on his contract, and was planning to retire anyway. But management fired him, and the only reason was that if he continued to play the way he has been for the past few games they'd owe him a ton of money for incentive clauses in his contract. The bastards."

"If he has a contract, they can't just fire him, can they?"

"As long as they can convince the doctor to say he's not healthy, they can do anything they damn well please. You saw the way he was limping. Hell, half of the professional football players have worse knees than that, but it's always a good excuse." He brooded for a few minutes. "And saying that he retired, as if it was voluntary. That's what really stinks."

When they pulled into the yard at the Greener Earth, Tess asked suddenly, "Do you have a column to do for tomorrow?"

He turned to her, his eyes glittering. "Yeah, I do. Why do you ask?"

She grinned. "I wondered if you were rehearsing."

His face gradually relaxed, and he finally smiled. "Thanks. I'll keep the editorializing where it belongs in the future."

As she swung out of the car, she said, "Please don't. I found it very instructive." She smiled at him. "I had no idea you were such an idealist, Nick."

"Yeah, well don't go spreading it around. It'd ruin my image." He gave her braid a tug and grinned at her as they walked through the door.

The office was deserted, and a glance at the clock

reminded Tess that she hadn't eaten lunch yet. She thought longingly of the Mexican restaurant that Donna had mentioned that morning. The stack of papers on her desk hadn't gotten any smaller, though, so she put the thought of tacos firmly out of her mind, sat down, and pulled her calculator toward her.

"Where is everybody?" Nick asked behind her.

"Out to lunch," she replied absently, already busy. "They went to that new Mexican place down the street, I think, so if you want to join them, go ahead."

"Aren't you hungry?" he asked in a puzzled voice.

"Hmmm. I've got too much to do here." He didn't answer, and when she heard the door close behind him, she didn't even look up.

Completely engrossed with her task, Tess lost track of time. When a slight breeze ruffled the hair at the nape of her neck, she absently rubbed her hand across the spot. It tickled her again, and her shoulders twitched. The third time, it jolted her to consciousness, and she whirled around in her chair.

Nick's blue eyes were inches from hers. "I thought I was going to have to resort to a kiss." His voice was low and seductive. Tess tried to scoot away, but her chair was firmly wedged between Nick and her desk.

Nick, watching her, murmured, "Maybe I will anyway." His lips moved closer to Tess's. As she watched him, her own lips tingled with anticipation. Her mouth opened slightly, then dropped open completely as Nick leaned around her and whispered a kiss on the back of her neck.

Before she could say anything, Nick jumped up and flourished a bag in front of her. "If it weren't for me, you'd waste away to nothing." He grinned at Tess's slightly puzzled look. "Lunch. Tacos, to be exact. You have to keep up your strength when you're wrestling with a calculator."

The tantalizing aroma coming from the bag Nick held made Tess's stomach suddenly gurgle. Tess snatched the bag away from him.

"My stomach seems to have said it all." She opened the bag and inhaled deeply. "Bartholomew, you just shot right up to the top of my list. I'm hungry enough to eat the horse and chase the driver."

Tess watched Nick as he walked to their small refrigerator to get two cans of soda. Just when she had made up her mind that he was lower than a bottom dwelling slug, he *would* have to do something thoughtful like get her lunch. Remembering again his kindness to Jack Abbott that morning, she grudgingly admitted that there was more to Nick Bartholomew than a smart mouth and a clever pen. She felt his breath in her hair again as she remembered that feathery kiss. So much for putting Nick Bartholomew out of her mind. Well, at least she could act like she was in control, and not let him see how much that careless kiss had affected her.

Tess deliberately pushed out of her mind the image of Nick's face poised inches from hers. "Thanks," she said as he handed her a cold can of cola. "I may decide I like being interviewed after all if all the reporters provide this kind of service."

"Nah, you don't want to talk to any of those other guys. Take it from me, they're all bums." He grinned at her skeptical look. "I ought to know. I play cards with most of them."

While they ate the tacos, Nick kept her howling with stories about the sports celebrities he'd interviewed. By the time they finished eating, Tess had forgotten that Nick was supposed to be interviewing her, too. She felt like she had been laughing with an old friend.

Tess took a long drink from the can of cola and stood up, reluctant to get back to her paperwork. "Want to go for a walk?" she asked Nick. "I need to check on the collection bins. There's been a steady stream of cars coming in all morning, and I want to make sure that they're not overflowing."

Nick didn't remind her that she had asked Mike to check the bins with her just a couple of hours ago. He had a feeling that she wouldn't be too happy if she realized that he'd seen their fight. He jumped up and opened the door for her. He'd use any excuse to spend a few more minutes with her. It was necessary for the interview, he assured himself.

The October sun warmed the asphalt as they strolled across the yard. Nick felt immediately that something was wrong, but couldn't put his finger on it. He looked around, puzzled. Then it hit him—it was quiet in the yard. There were no truck engines rumbling, no sound of glass breaking and tin cans rattling, no voices shouting. He looked at Tess, a question in his eyes.

"A minor lull in the action. It's pretty startling, isn't it?" She smiled. "I've never gotten used to it. I'm so used to the noise and commotion that when it's quiet like this I feel like I'm in the wrong place."

Tess peered into the open end of the giant metal box that held the newspapers for recycling. They were stacked in neat rows up to the ceiling, and they filled only half the box. She looked over her shoulder at Nick. "Plenty of room in here," she called cheerfully.

Tess backed out and walked over to the bins that held the glass. These, too, were giant metal boxes, but instead of being open on one end, they were open at the top. She climbed the stairs next to the first one, peered inside, then checked the next two. Satisfied, she walked back to where Nick stood.

"Plenty of room in all of them," she reported happily. Seeing Nick's slightly baffled look, she gestured toward the containers.

"Nothing seems to upset recyclers as much as bins that are full and overflowing. We try to keep ours almost empty—it seems to make the people think that they need to hurry back with more cans and glass and newspaper to fill up those bins for us."

She grinned at Nick. "That's one of our secret weapons, you know. You just better not go and reveal our tricks in your column."

"My lips, as they say, are sealed," Nick promised solemnly.

As they started to walk back toward the office, they passed another bin, a long, low metal container with several small closed doors. "Hey, you forgot to check this one," Nick called as he strode over and pulled up one of the doors.

Tess opened her mouth to shout at Nick to stop, but no sound would come out. She stood rooted to the spot, watching Nick in horror. Sure enough, there were the bees, buzzing angrily out of the bin and certainly headed straight for her. Her mind told her to walk away, slowly, but her feet refused to move.

"This one's only half full, too," Nick called with satisfaction. He let the lid bang down, and turned back toward Tess.

She stood there, white-faced and trembling. Her eyes were huge, the pupils dilated so much that they seemed like black pools. She looked like every one of her worst nightmares had just materialized in front of her.

"Tess?" he whispered, shocked. "What's wrong?"

She licked her lips once and opened her mouth. A small, high pitched sound came out. It didn't even remotely resemble a human voice.

In two long strides he reached her and dragged her into his arms. Tess wrapped her arms around him and clung. She buried her face in his shoulder and held on. Nick rocked her slowly, comforting her, until the trembling lessened. After a few moments, Tess raised her head to say urgently, "I have to get away from here."

Without a word, Nick draped an arm over her shoulders and steered her back to the office. Once they were inside, he sat her down in her chair and, still without saying anything, got her a glass of water. She drank it down, then set the glass on her desk, thankful that her hand was shaking only slightly.

"Thank you, Nick," she said in a low voice. "You must think I'm a total idiot."

"Tess." His voice was honey pouring over her. "You know better than that by now. What happened, for God's sake?"

"Didn't you see them?" Tess was astonished.

"See who?"

"The bees, of course," she said impatiently.

"What bees?" Nick was totally confused by now.

"The bees that came swarming out of the metal bin when you opened it." Her voice shook slightly as she spoke.

"Tess, there wasn't any swarm of bees," Nick began, but stopped abruptly when he saw Tess cringe.

"Hey, I'm sorry." He crouched next to her, taking both of her cold hands in his. "I had no idea you were so scared of bees."

She laughed shakily. "Saying I'm scared of bees is like saying that the Pacific Ocean is just a little puddle. I'm totally, completely, irrationally petrified of bees." She drew in a shuddering breath. "This time of year, they're always hanging around the empty cans. For most people they're just a minor annoyance, but I can't go anywhere near that bin without freaking out."

She ran her fingers through her hair, pulling even more strands out of the braid, willing herself to stop shaking. She always hated to lose control, and it particularly galled her that it had happened in front of Nick. He must think she was a complete fool. Well, she'd just have to forget about the damn bees and get back to work. She was reaching for a stack of papers when one of the computers behind her let out a sudden whine, and she jumped half way out of her chair.

"There's nothing to be ashamed of, you know." Tess whirled around and stared at Nick. "Personally, even thinking about rats makes me queasy. It must have scared the hell out of you when I opened that lid and you saw those yellowjackets flying out."

Thinking about it had Tess shaking all over again. She looked down at her hands in her lap. They were clenched into fists, and as she looked at them she deliberately relaxed her fingers.

"When I was a kid, I stepped on a bumblebee nest once. I was playing in my backyard, and the next thing I knew there were hundreds of bees buzzing around me. I guess I ran for the house, because my mother told me she found me hysterical in a corner of the kitchen. I was really lucky; I only got stung a few times. Ever since, though ..." Tess shrugged her shoulders and tried to smile. "I guess I should have warned you about that bin. Nobody ever goes near it when I'm around, and it didn't even occur to me that you would open it. Thanks for rescuing me." She paused and looked away. "I hope I didn't make you too uncomfortable."

"Tess." Nick reached over and ran a finger lightly down her cheek. "Don't be silly. I can't say you don't make me uncomfortable, but it has nothing to do with the bees."

His voice was a low, caressing murmur. Tess looked at him, and swallowed. His meaning was all too clear. She tried to look away, knew she had to look away, but stared, mesmerized, as Nick leaned over and cupped her face between his hands.

Later, she couldn't remember which of them moved first. Somehow she was in his arms and his lips were on hers, seeking, demanding, but giving as much as he asked. She shivered, but there was no thought of bees in her mind now. The hard muscles in his back quivered, then tensed beneath her fingers. Groaning, Nick ran his hand down her back and over the curve of her hip, cupping her closer to him. His fingers lingered at the junction of her hip and thigh, gently caressing until Tess moaned into his mouth.

If he let her go now, she thought hazily, she would slide bonelessly to the floor.

She was on fire, burning at every place Nick's body touched hers. When Nick's hand skimmed her inner thigh, the fire centered in her stomach and burned downward. Her tongue twined with his and she savored the dark, velvet taste of him.

Nick lifted his mouth from hers, only to glide his lips over her neck and shoulder. When his tongue circled her collarbone and his fingers opened the top button on her blouse, she started to tremble. Using every last ounce of willpower she possessed, she laid her hand over his and stopped his fingers.

"No, Nick, please." Her voice was trembling as much as her body.

He immediately let go of the button, but instead of letting her go he wrapped his arms around her and rested his chin on her head. Tess felt his body shuddering as he took deep breaths. After a minute, he put his hands on her shoulders and ran them lightly down her arms to hold her hands.

"Tess," Nick began, then shook his head. "I'm not going to apologize for this. I'm not the least bit sorry it happened." He grasped Tess's hands more tightly as she tried to pull away.

"Look," he said, caressing her palms with his thumbs, "I'm not going to say I'm sorry every time I kiss you." She opened her mouth to answer, but he spoke first. "Yes, I lied this morning. And we both knew I was lying. Just like we both know this is going to happen again."

Tess tried again to pull her hands away from Nick's grasp. "The only thing that's happening between us is lust. Your hormones are calling to my hormones and that's all it is. What you don't understand is that we're not going to act on it."

Nick released her hands, but continued to stand in

front of her, forcing her to look at him. "There's more than lust involved here, Tess," he said quietly.

"Nick, we barely know each other. We're involved in an adversary relationship right now, and I feel like I have to analyze everything I say to you. I have no idea what you think about me, but I don't trust you at all. Now tell me how what we're feeling could be anything more than simple lust."

Nick moved back and sat on the edge of Tess's desk. The sight of his long, lean legs stretched out in front of him made Tess swallow once. Nick held her gaze for a long moment, until she looked away. "I'm not sure what I call it, but there's nothing simple about what I feel about you," he said softly.

He glanced out the window and saw that Mike and Donna were walking across the yard. "This isn't, however, the time to pursue it." He stood up and strolled over to Donna's desk, where he picked up the magazine he had been reading earlier.

"Why didn't you tell me that the Greener Earth was going to be moving?"

"What?" Tess was completely confused by the abrupt change of subject.

"Mike asked you earlier if you were still going to be here next month, and I assumed that he meant you were moving sometime soon."

"No, that's not what he meant." Tess's words were clipped and final. She deliberately turned away from Nick and sat down at her desk. Nick immediately plopped himself back down on the corner of it and leaned toward her.

"Well, what's the story, then? Are you guys having problems, or something?"

Tess looked at him them. "I don't think that's any of your business, Mr. Bartholomew," she said coldly.

"Hey, babe, anything that involves you for this week is my business," he answered, very deliberately.

Tess didn't stop to think that he was goading her, trying to get a rise out of her. She didn't remind herself to be careful, to think about what she was saying. She simply reacted.

"Listen, Bartholomew, what goes on here is nobody's business but Mike's and mine. I told you up front that my business was off limits as far as your article was concerned. If you're going to eavesdrop on private conversations, you can just get the hell out of here right now."

Nick stood up lazily, a slight smile on his face. "I'd be happy to, Tess. If you want to write me that check for fifty thousand dollars, I'll take it with me. Made payable to the Post, of course."

Tess jumped up, oblivious to Mike and Donna, who had just walked in the door. "You can go straight to hell, you scum-sucking worm," she shouted. She spotted Nick's notebook, which was sitting on her desk. She picked it up and threw it at him. It hit him squarely in the chest and fell to the floor. "And take that with you!"

"Too bad, Donna, it looks like we missed all the fun," Mike said in a loud voice. He looked at Nick, who was standing staring at Tess with a smug look on his face. "Don't be so pleased with yourself. I'd be relieved that was all she had on her desk. The last time she threw something, it was a coffee mug." He smiled happily at the memory. "Heavy sucker, too. Hit the guy right on the forehead. It was the last time that thug tried to threaten us." He looked meaningfully at Nick.

Nick turned his head and looked at Mike, his eyes challenging. "This is a private fight. I don't think Tess needs your help."

"Believe me, I'm not trying to get in the middle of anything. Just offering you a little friendly advice." Back off, his eyes said.

Tess watched the two men eye each other. They reminded her of two small boys circling in the dust before wrestling each other to the ground. "Stop it, both of you."

She walked over to Mike and touched his cheek. "Thanks, partner, but I think Nick and I will take this outside."

Tess felt like she was riding the tilt-a-whirl. The bees, then the kiss she'd shared with Nick, then the questions about the Center had thrown her from one emotional extreme to another. What she needed was a nice hole to hide in for a while. She walked out the door with Nick right behind her.

Tess turned to Nick and took a deep breath. "I'm sorry. I had no right to get angry with you for just doing your job."

The words quivered between them like a pitchfork thrown into the ground. Your job to find my secrets, my job to hide them from you. Was this her way of distilling her complicated feelings about Nick down to something more easily dismissed, she wondered suddenly? She thrust the thought away, not wanting to examine it. It's time, she told herself, that this relationship centered around business, anyway.

She looked back at Nick, catching him staring at her. His expression was unreadable, flat and even.

"Can we just forget about this for now, please?"

"Consider the subject dropped, Tess."

For now, his eyes added.

# CHAPTER FIVE

Tess rubbed the towel vigorously over her hair, then paused and frowned. Yes, the phone was definitely ringing. Wrapping the towel around her, she ran into her bedroom and picked it up.

"Oh no, Mike, not today," she groaned. "Are you sure that conference can't be postponed?" She listened for a moment more, then sighed. "Yeah, I know how important it is." She paused to listen again. "All right. I'll get myself psyched to pick up garbage. I guess I should at least thank you for giving me some warning." She glanced out her window and remembered the heavy, humidity laden air. Every breath had been an effort during her run that morning, and she knew it would only get worse as the day went on. It was going to be one long, miserable day driving that truck.

She hung up the phone and walked back into the bathroom, combing her hair with her fingers. Suddenly she grinned. There was one redeeming feature about having to drive one of the collection routes today. Nick would have to do it with her if he was really determined to stick to her like glue. The sight of Nick Bartholomew tossing cans and glass into a recycling truck would almost make the day worthwhile. Almost, but not quite.

Tess scowled at herself in the mirror. This wasn't the

first time in the last twelve hours her mind had conjured up Nick Bartholomew. Her sleep had been disturbed by vivid, erotic dreams, all starring Nick. She'd gotten up early and run much farther than usual, hoping to erase his image from her mind. Even at the end of her run, she thought disgustedly, when she'd been gasping for breath and wobbly legged, the first thing she looked for when she reached her drive was Nick's car.

Like she told him yesterday, it was nothing more than a bad case of hormones. If she could get through the rest of the week, he'd be gone and she could forget all about smooth, sexy Nick Bartholomew. She scowled at herself again. If she couldn't convince herself, how did she ever expect Nick to believe her?

Tess rummaged in a drawer, looking for her oldest, most tattered jeans. Finding a pair that even Goodwill would have rejected, she pulled them on and looked for a T-shirt. Even though it was the middle of October, it was already very warm outside. Combined with the humidity, Tess knew she was in for an uncomfortable day. Finally she dragged on an old Rolling Stones shirt that was as faded and soft as a well-used baby blanket. She looked down at herself and smiled reluctantly. This wasn't exactly what they had in mind when they said to dress for success.

Being comfortable while driving the truck was at least half the battle, Tess reminded herself as she started her coffee. As committed as she was to recycling, she hated to actually drive the routes and pick up the bottles, cans, and newspapers. She always felt like she'd been rolling around in a dumpster by the end of the day, and even a long shower couldn't quite get rid of the grubby feeling. The men and women who drove the Greener Earth's recycling trucks were well paid for their efforts. As far as Tess was concerned, they earned every penny.

She lingered over her coffee and newspaper for longer than usual, trying to postpone the inevitable. Guilt finally pushed her out the door and into her car. The other person on her route today would be waiting for her, impatient to get started. She might as well get it over with.

The first thing she noticed as she stopped her car was Nick's sports car parked behind the office. The butterflies suddenly fluttering in her stomach must have been wearing boots. Size twelves, at least. She couldn't possibly face Nick after yesterday. Even now, thinking about the way she had yelled at him and thrown his notebook at his chest was enough to make her blush. Not to mention that kiss. Tess sighed. It was shaping up to be quite a day.

"Good morning, Nick." Tess was surprised that her voice sounded so normal.

" 'Morning, Tess." Nick looked up from the newspaper he was reading and gave her his lazy smile. "Glad to see you could make it this morning."

How could he act so, so ... *normal,* after yesterday? Tess shook her head. The man was a mystery to her. She glanced at the clock then and realized how late she was. "I'm allowed to get here late because I'm going to work harder today than all of you combined," she retorted with a smile.

She looked at Nick and the smile slowly turned into a grin. "Except maybe you, Bartholomew."

Tess scrutinized Nick's clothes. The pleated gray flannel pants and yellow polo shirt looked terrific, but weren't exactly suitable for garbage collecting. "I sure hope you have some other clothes with you, Nick. I'd really hate to see what you're wearing get ruined."

Nick leaned closer and murmured, "Just what did you have in mind, anyway?"

Nick's meaning was only too clear. Feeling her face flushing crimson, Tess opened her mouth to reply, then shut it again. What was wrong with her this morning? Since when could a man make her lose her cool like this? She dragged her mind back to business.

"If you want to come with me today, you're going to have to change your clothes," she pointed out sweetly. "I have to do a collection route because one of the drivers is sick.  You can stay here, of course, but I thought you might want to see what we really do."

Nick looked at her suspiciously.  "What do my clothes have to do with coming with you?"

In spite of herself, Tess grinned again.  "I'm not dressed in these," she indicated her torn jeans and old shirt, "just for the sake of elegance. This is garbage we're picking up, you know."

"I'm not sure I like the sound of that 'we,' " Nick answered warily.

"Anyone that rides the truck is expected to help out, including reporters." She laughed out loud. "Especially reporters."

Nick stared at her for a moment, until his lips curled into a reluctant answering grin. "Why do I have the feeling that you know something that I don't?"

"You have five minutes to change your clothes, Bartholomew, so you better get busy." Tess spoke over her shoulder as she was walking out the door. She had managed to get through that without disgracing herself, Tess thought. If she could make it through the rest of the day without any other incidents, she would have all evening and the rest of the night to put Nick firmly out of her mind. The problem was, she was afraid that she was the one who was out of her mind

\*\*\*

Tess glanced at Nick as she wiped her face with her bandana. "Real glamorous job, isn't it?"

Nick looked over at her and grimaced.  "I have to admit, I'm sure there've been times when I've felt more dirty, but I can't remember any of them right now." He sighed and wiped the sweat off his forehead with his arm.

They walked behind the truck to the next house, and Tess bent to pick up the red plastic crate.  Reaching in, they tossed bottles and cans into the proper compartments in the back of the truck. Both of them wore gloves, but as the containers flew toward the truck, the last bits of liquid left in them splattered their arms and chests. After a couple of blocks, Tess always felt like someone had poured a can of Coke over her head, then followed it with a beer chaser. Today was no exception, and the stifling heat and humidity just made her more uncomfortable.

Tossing the plastic container back onto the ground, Tess slapped the truck to signal the driver to move forward. As they trudged to the next house, Nick said, "You know, Tess, you're opening up whole new worlds for me. Worlds I have absolutely no desire to know about, let alone be on such intimate terms with." He shook his head. "This is definitely one week I'm not going to forget."

Tess glanced over at him. He wore the same red T-shirt and navy blue sweat pants he'd worn the first time they'd run together. Now, however, they were covered with blotches of different colored, sticky liquids. Sweat had plastered his shirt to his back, and his bare arms were dotted with stray bits of what looked like tomatoes and cat food. She would have laughed, but she knew she looked just as bad.

"Yes, this does tend to stick in your memory." Tess threw down another crate and wiped her face again. "And on your clothes, in your hair, and under your fingernails."

The truck stopped at the corner, and Tess walked toward the cab. "Come on, Nick, it's our turn to drive."

The young man who had been driving the truck swung out and planted a baseball cap backwards on his head. Taking in the mess on Tess's clothing, he grinned appreciatively and strolled toward the next red crate. Tess settled behind the wheel and eased the clutch out. The truck turned the corner and rumbled down the street, the bottles breaking and the cans clanking every time they hit a bump. "There's a jug of water under the dashboard over there." She pointed toward a blue cooler. "Help yourself and pass it over."

She heard Nick gulping from the thermos, and stopped at the first house just as he handed her the bottle. Lifting it to her mouth, she felt Nick's eyes on her. She turned to look at him as she drank, and his taste, left behind on the rim of the thermos, caressed her tongue. The sharp, sweaty flavor exploded in her mouth and filled her senses.

Her eyes locked with Nick's. One of them was breathing heavily, or maybe it was both of them. His fingers trailed down her cheek, then captured a drop of water from her lips. When he licked it off his fingertip, desire exploded along her nerves and pounded in her blood.

"Hey, Tess, you got sunstroke, or what? Get it in gear!" She jumped at the voice in her ear. Red faced, she turned to the man hanging onto the door of the truck.

"Sorry, Tony, I guess I didn't hear you."

"How many times do I gotta hit this thing before you get the idea? Let's go!"

Tony jumped off the truck as Tess, her cheeks still scarlet, fumbled with the gearshift. She could feel the sweat trickle down her back as the truck jerked forward and moved slowly down the street. Even before they stopped at the next house, she heard the bottles and cans crashing into the bins.

Glancing over at Nick, she was startled to see him looking as uncomfortable as she felt. He must have noticed her surprise, because he gave her a faint smile. "I'm not crazy about an audience, either." Then he began to chuckle. "But at least I'm not the boss.

"Speaking of which," he continued, with a curious look, "is that the way all your employees talk to you?"

Tess listened carefully for the slap on the truck, then moved slowly forward. Turning to Nick again, she said, "It's kind of an unwritten law on the truck that everyone's equal." She shrugged. "Besides, Tony was right. He shouldn't have to stand around while we ..." Her face reddened again and she looked away.

The silence stretched out for several minutes as Tess concentrated on driving the truck. Finally Nick asked, "How did you manage to end up with this job today, anyway?"

"Simple. Everyone else had an excuse. The woman who normally collects with Tony is sick. Mike was presenting a bid for routes to the city council of Orrington. Steve, who coordinates the trucks and supervises the drivers, was interviewing people today. That left me, and here we are."

"How often do you have to do this?" He sounded genuinely interested, and Tess noticed that his tape recorder was nowhere in sight.

"Too often," she said emphatically. "When we got our first route, nobody else worked for us, and Mike and I did all the collecting ourselves. Believe me, I got my fill those first few months. I don't have to do this very often anymore, but I still hate every minute of it."

As she finished speaking, she pulled the truck over to the curb. "Come on, Nick, back to work."

"You mean we have to do that again?"

He sounded so horrified that Tess laughed. "Hey, we're just getting started."

***

"I don't want to point any fingers, but one of you is very ripe." Nick leaned against the seat of the truck, his elbow resting on the open window.

Tess, sandwiched in the middle between Tony and Nick, opened her eyes and sniffed the air. "You're no prize yourself, Bartholomew."

Leaning forward to look at Nick, Tony added, "Yeah, newspaperman, I wouldn't stay outside too long today. The flies will be all over you like ugly on an ape."

Nick turned to Tess. "How do you do it? My butt was dragging after a couple of hours, but you looked like you could have kept going indefinitely."

She stretched and shrugged. "I'm just used to it, I guess. Besides, Tony nags if I don't keep up."

Draping his arm across Tess's shoulder, Tony shook his head. "Don't let her feed you a line. She may be the boss, but this one works harder than the rest of them combined."

Laughing, she lightly punched Tony's shoulder. "Except Tony, of course."

"Hey, that goes without sayin'."

By the time they got back to the yard, Tess felt like something the cat had looked over and rejected. Never in her whole life had she felt so slimy. She eased herself out of the truck and headed for the office, intent on scraping off the worst of the debris.

Nick caught up with her just as she walked in the door. "Where are you rushing off to?"

"To soap and warm water. I want to make sure this stuff hasn't permanently changed my skin color." She raised her eyebrows at him. "Care to join me?"

He grinned. "That's the best offer I've had in a long, long time."

As they toweled their arms and hands dry. Tess glanced at Nick. "I know where Mike keeps some clean clothes." She looked him up and down. "You're taller than he is, and not as heavy, but at least you'll be able to get home without ruining your car's upholstery."

"I would kiss your feet for clean clothes," he answered fervently. "But are you sure you don't want to use them yourself?"

She grinned. "I keep my own stash. In this business, you learn early to have an extra set of clothes handy."

Tess emerged from the bathroom a little later dressed in baggy shorts and an old red shirt to see Nick sitting on the edge of her desk, legs swinging, drinking a Coke. He was barefoot, as she was, but the legs of his jeans ended at mid-calf. When he stood up to hand her a can of cola, she burst out laughing. The waist of Mike's jeans was apparently much too large for him, so he'd tied a piece of baling twine around them to hold them up. Combined with the too-short pants legs and the bare feet, the overall effect was not exactly one of debonair sophistication.

"You can laugh," Nick pointed out, "but at least I don't smell like tuna surprise."

"All right," she agreed, still chuckling, "we'll call it a draw."

They drank their sodas in companionable silence. Tess felt oddly reluctant to go home, even though every pore on her body screamed for a shower. She'd enjoyed Nick's company today, she realized. Collecting the recyclables was still a messy, dirty, smelly job, but having him working with her had made it almost tolerable. She tried not to think about other things she would find far more pleasurable with Nick.

"You know, Tess," Nick's voice interrupted her thoughts, "I'd like to talk to you about running. Can we get together tonight?"

She hesitated. She wanted to refuse, but knew that Nick's request was reasonable. After all, that was the reason he was here. Reluctantly, she said, "I guess that would be okay. Why don't we meet back at my house?"

"Great. As soon as I clean up, I'll be there." He looked down at himself and laughed. "If I don't show up until tomorrow, I'm sure you'll understand why."

Tess locked the door and they walked slowly to their cars. She unlocked the door of the Toyota and was about to get in when something caught her eye. "Oh no," she groaned, leaning against the car. She looked again, hoping it had been an optical illusion, but the tire was still flat. "Not today, of all days."

Nick walked over and looked at it. "Yep, it's flat, all right. Well, get the jack and let's get started."

"There's a little problem with the jack." Tess stared at the tire, as if she could will it to reinflate. "It's not in my car."

"Where exactly is it?"

"I suppose it's in Donna's car. She borrowed it last week."

"Tess." Nick's voice was very quiet. "Didn't anyone ever tell you that you're supposed to keep your jack in your car?"

"I've had other things on my mind this week besides getting my jack back from Donna," she flashed at him. "Look, you go on home. I'll call Donna and have her bring it over."

Nick said impatiently, "I'm not going to leave you here by yourself with a flat tire to fix." He ran his fingers through his hair. "Why don't you just come with me? We can stop by my apartment first so I can get cleaned up, then we'll go to your house. I can fix dinner while you take a shower." When she hesitated, he added, "It's the only logical thing to do."

"All right, I guess that makes sense." She thought about a shower and suppressed a sigh. She supposed it wouldn't kill her to wait a little longer to clean up, even if she did smell like something that had died last week.

Tess leaned back against the seat of the car as Nick drove through the rush hour traffic. She closed her eyes and inhaled the rich scent of the leather upholstery. The sports car's engine purred, relaxing her. It had been a long, tiring day.

Opening her eyes with a start, she realized that the engine noise had stopped.

Nick opened her door and reached in a hand to help her out. She slid out and looked around, recognizing where she was immediately. The Lakes was an apartment complex famous for its "swinging singles" lifestyle. The buildings were set among rolling hills; there were several lakes where the residents sailed, and there was even a small ski hill that was always crowded in the winter.

Nick's building was one that was set back from the road, surrounded by trees. It would be a great apartment with a beautiful view, she suspected. All the magazines that had written up The Lakes apartment complex as a unique and lovely place to live had said so.

When they walked into Nick's apartment, her suspicions were confirmed. One wall was floor to ceiling windows, and all she could see was trees in every shade of autumn. The apartment itself seemed to be an extension of the spectacular view, with furniture made out of massive pieces of wood and brightly colored cushions. A rug with an intricate, Indian pattern covered the hardwood floor, and plants lurked in the corners of the room.

"This is beautiful." She turned to Nick and found him watching her.

"I'm glad you like it."

Gazing around, she said lightly, "I've always wanted to see what one of these apartments looked like."

"One of what apartments?" He sounded bewildered.

"You know, one of the places where 'they' live."

"Maybe I missed something here, but who are 'they?' "

"Don't play the innocent with me. You know, the sexy, scandalous swinging singles, the people with soap opera lives." She tried, but couldn't quite keep the laughter out of her voice.

When she looked at him, he was smiling, but as their eyes met his smile faded. "I can see I'm going to have to convince you that I can be quite serious."

Somehow he'd moved so he stood in front of her. Move away, her saner voice sternly commanded, but Tess just stared at him, mesmerized. Slowly he reached out a hand and traced the line of her jaw. One finger, and her skin was on fire. Tess looked at his hand and licked her lips. Those sensitive, gentle fingers were whispering over her face and throat, burning every place they touched.

"Nick," she breathed.

He touched his finger to her lips. "Shh," he murmured, "not a word." Cupping his hand behind her head, he drew her nearer. "Just one kiss, Tess."

His lips touched hers, lightly, then pulled away. With an inarticulate murmur, Tess stepped closer, reaching a tentative hand to Nick's face. He groaned, crushing her against him.

All trace of her saner self vanished, consumed in the flames. She was drowning in Nick, in the taste and feel of him. His tongue traced her lips, then parted them and slowly explored the velvet darkness of her mouth.

Desire burned in her stomach and sizzled through her blood. Her hands traced the ridges of muscle up and down his back, feeling them tense under her fingers. Just when she thought she would never take another breath, Nick tore his mouth away and leaned his forehead against hers.

"Tess," he groaned, "Oh, God, Tess." With a trembling hand, he pushed some loose strands of hair away from her face. "You make me want too much," he whispered.

Then his mouth was on hers again, demanding a response. Answering him, demanding of him in return, Tess felt herself falling, spinning out of control. She opened her eyes to look at Nick, and found they were lying on the floor. Nick's body was half covering hers, his legs wedged between hers. His hand stroked down her side, and she felt her nipples tighten with anticipation.

She slipped her hand beneath his shirt and felt his abdomen quiver and tense at her touch. Roaming upward, her fingers tangled in the soft hair and brushed over a flat nipple. When he suddenly jerked, she drew away, startled.

"Please," he said hoarsely, "don't stop." Laying her hand on his chest again, she slowly ran her fingers over him, feeling the curls comb through her fingers.

He groaned again and gently pulled her hand from his chest. Holding both her hands easily above her head with one of his, he lightly touched one of her nipples through the soft cotton shirt. Watching it harden, he lowered his head and captured the soft peak with his mouth. Even through the rough material, the sensation made every nerve in her body cry out.

Watching her face, Nick slowly raised the T-shirt and pulled it over her head. The cool air against her bare skin was like a dash of cold water. Tess's bra had been discarded along with the rest of her dirty clothes, and she felt terribly exposed. She moved instinctively to cover herself, but Nick tightened his hold on her hands.

"Don't, please. You're so beautiful, more than I ever imagined." A twinkle appeared in his eyes. "And believe me, I imagined plenty."

Tess felt the heat flood her cheeks, and Nick chuckled. "Haven't you thought about me?" he teased. When she blushed even harder, he laughed out loud.

Letting go of her, he rolled over so that she was on top of him. He reached down and with one fluid movement pulled off his own T-shirt, then pulled her against him. The soft mat of Nick's hair tickled her nipples, making her shiver. Then his mouth was on hers again, and her blood pounded with every heartbeat. All thought of stopping, of being sensible, had long since vanished. Her arms were wrapped around Nick's neck, pressing him closer to her.

His fingers were finding every sensitive spot on her back and sides, trailing up and down with a feathery touch. She moaned his name, and the sound whispered into his mouth. His arms tightened around her momentarily, then one hand slid down her back to press her bottom and urge her closer.

Nick's other hand glided down her leg until his fingers found the delicate skin of her inner thigh. Burrowing under the baggy material of her shorts, his hand circled upward, barely skimming her leg. When he reached the apex of her thighs, he cupped her in his palm.

Tess's whole body shuddered, then tensed. Her

instinctive movement away from his hand made Nick freeze. His hand was still for a moment, then slowly glided down her leg again and smoothed up her back. His touch was gentle and reassuring now, not passion-heavy and demanding. Tess felt him tremble, then he wrapped his arms around her and held her quietly.

Tess's body was still humming with desire. She raised her head and looked at Nick, a question in her eyes.

"God, Tess, don't look at me that way." His voice was ragged, as if he was having trouble breathing. "It's hard enough to stop, without you looking at me like that." He rolled over again, and raised himself up on his elbows as he looked down at her.

"You were right," he said softly as he ran a finger down her face. "You don't really know me, and I have a job to do. When we make love, it won't be because we got carried away by our hormones on the living room floor. It'll be because we both want to make love."

He sat up abruptly and looked around. Spotting her T-shirt, he silently handed it to her and reached for his own. Tess concentrated on getting her shirt on and tucking it into her shorts. She couldn't bring herself to meet Nick's eyes. Even though her body still throbbed, her mind was now crystal clear. Thank goodness one of them had still been able to think!

She smoothed her hands nervously over her hair and down her braid. Its stiffness reminded her that she hadn't showered after picking up the trash. My God, what had she been thinking about? Looking anywhere but at Nick, frantically trying to think of something to say, she finally murmured, "Your rug is never going to be the same."

She could feel his eyes on her. "Neither am I," he answered softly. He took her chin in his hand and gently turned her until she was looking at him.

"I don't understand this, either, you know." At her startled look, he smiled ironically. "The last thing, the very last thing I had in mind when I got this assignment, was getting involved with you." Reaching out a hand, he tucked a few loose strands of hair behind her ear. "To tell the truth, I had already decided I wouldn't even like you." He leaned forward and gave her a quick, hard kiss. "Just proves how wrong I can be."

Tess looked down at their joined hands. "I don't know what to think, Nick," she finally said in a low voice. "I'm not even sure if I trust you, but I ... I mean we ..." she stumbled to a halt.

"Can you at least believe me if I say I would never deliberately hurt you?" he asked quietly.

She took a fraction of a second too long to answer. "No, I don't think you would." *But you could wound me fatally without even realizing it,* she thought. The emotions he stirred in her were frightening, to say the least. She felt control of the situation slipping out of her hands, and it was terrifying. It was like taking a step and feeling nothing beneath your feet, knowing you were spinning down into an abyss and bracing for the final, fatal impact.

"There are only five more days left in your contract with the Post. We'll talk about this again six days from now." Watching her, Nick ran his hand down the side of her face. He picked up her hand again and pressed a kiss into the palm, making her shiver once more. Then, in another of his disconcerting shifts, he jumped up and hauled her to her feet. "I don't know about you, but I think I'd better take that shower. The plants in here look like they're beginning to wilt from the aroma."

He took a step away from her, then turned and said, with a glint in his eye, "Care to join me?"

She shook her head, trying to act casual. "No thanks. I'll just keep away from the plants and I shouldn't do too much damage."

Grinning, he asked, "Are you sure? I could wash those hard to reach places on your back."

Trying not to laugh, she said, "It's a tempting offer, but I'll have to decline."

---

He gave an exaggerated shrug. "It's your loss."

When she heard the water start to run, she sat down and picked up a magazine. The next thing she knew, Nick was shaking her shoulder and calling her name. "Come on, Tess, it's time to go."

Opening her eyes, she saw his face right above hers. He smiled at her and said, "Come on, sleepyhead. Time to get you home."

Tess stumbled to her feet, trying to clear the fuzz out of her brain. Nick draped an arm across her shoulders and guided her through the door.

After she had settled into her seat in his car and they started off, she said, "Sorry, Nick, I think I'm going to have to reschedule the next installment of our interview. I'm beat."

He flicked a quick grin at her. "I figured that when it took me five minutes to wake you up." He changed lanes smoothly, then turned to her again. "Tomorrow's Saturday. Do you have to go in to work?"

"I usually stop in for a while in the morning, just to make sure there aren't any problems. Other than that, no."

"Well, why don't we plan on doing this tomorrow, then?"

She hesitated. At least at work there was some structure, something else to do. She didn't know how she would survive a day in his company without something to keep them on a businesslike track. She was afraid she wanted to find out.

"Okay, I guess that would be all right."

He shot her a glance. "Don't sound so enthused. I might think you actually wanted to spend some time with me, or something."

In spite of herself, her mouth curved. "Particularly 'or something.' "

Tess leaned her head against the cushion and they rode the rest of the way in silence. When they reached her house, she opened the door and got out. Looking back in the car to say good-bye to Nick, she was surprised to see him standing next to her. "I want to make sure you don't fall asleep between here and the front door."

She turned the key in the lock and looked at Nick. "I'll see you tomorrow. Is nine o'clock all right?"

"Great. I'll see you then." Watching her face, Nick took her hand. "Five days, Tess." It was both a warning and a promise. He pressed a gentle kiss on her lips and was gone.

*** 

The message light was blinking on his answering machine when Nick walked back into his apartment. He pushed the button and listened to a message from his sister, complaining that the only time she heard from him was when she read his column in the paper. Grinning, he went into the kitchen to make a sandwich while he listened to the rest of his messages.

He only half heard Arnie's voice wondering if he still worked for the Post, since they hadn't had the pleasure of his company lately. Then he heard Jim Krieg's voice. Jim had found some information about Tess Phillips during his research that Nick would be very interested in.

Nick's stomach churned as he dialed Jim's number. "Hi, Jim, it's me. What do you have?"

The sandwich turned to ashes in his mouth as he listened to Jim. Finally he said, "Yeah, thanks, Jim. Yeah, I'll let you know."

Nick stared at the phone for a long time. Suddenly, swearing under his breath, he jumped up and drove his fist into the wall. Staring sightlessly at the depression in the plaster, he turned and walked out of the room.

# CHAPTER SIX

Tess set her coffee cup on the table and glanced at her watch again. It must be fast, she decided. There was no other possible explanation for the way the hands were rushing toward nine o'clock. Sighing, she stood up and carried her mug over to the sink. Nick would be here in less than ten minutes, that was certain. One thing she could say for him, he was at least prompt.

Throwing herself down on the living room couch, she picked up the morning newspaper and glanced at the headlines. She stared at the words telling of another important event in Eastern Europe without really seeing them. All she saw was Nick's face staring back at her, his dark blue eyes heavy lidded with passion, his lips poised over hers. Tossing the paper onto the floor in disgust, she leaned her head against the back of the couch and closed her eyes.

Yes, he was the sexiest man she had ever met. Yes, the gentleness and caring she glimpsed beneath his cynical exterior was heart melting. Yes, she admitted reluctantly, she was infatuated with him.

No, she told herself firmly as she opened her eyes, she was not falling in love with Nick Bartholomew. He was a dangerous man. He could destroy the Greener Earth with a few well chosen words, and she had to be constantly on her guard to make sure he didn't discover their secrets. How could you fall in love with someone when you didn't trust them as far as you could throw them? Pleased with her logic, she glanced out the window and saw Nick striding up the sidewalk.

Now, if only she could stop her heart from pounding like a piston whenever she saw him, Tess reflected, she might actually believe she had a chance against Nick Bartholomew.

She stood up and walked slowly to the door. This is a business appointment, she reminded herself. This is strictly to discuss running techniques and training habits. Hadn't they agreed last night that the personal had no place in this relationship, at least for the next five days? Yeah, right.

"Good morning, Nick." Tess closed the door behind him and said, too brightly, "How about some coffee?"

"Sounds great." He walked into the kitchen and poured himself a cup. Tess followed and poured another cup for herself, then sat down opposite him at the kitchen table.

She watched him, puzzled, as he managed to look everywhere but at her. The seconds stretched into a minute, then two, without either of them speaking. Tess's hands tightened around the coffee mug as she frantically tried to think of something innocuous to say. The silence was so palpable it beat against her ears.

"Um, is something wrong, Nick?"

He looked at her then. "Sorry. I'm just tired, I guess." He stared at her as if trying to read her thoughts. "I didn't sleep real well last night."

"Oh." If that was supposed to remind her of the previous evening, it worked all too well. Remembering how it had felt to lay on the floor all tangled up with him, her blood started to heat. She rose quickly and dumped her coffee in the sink. "Why don't we get going?"

Turning around, she was surprised to see a flash of

anger in his eyes. It disappeared so suddenly that after a moment she decided she'd been mistaken. He raised his mug and swallowed the rest of his coffee, then stood up. "Let's go."

The uncomfortable silence continued as they drove to the Greener Earth. Tess glanced over at him and saw his hands clenched on the steering wheel, his jaw tense.

"Are you sure everything's all right? You're acting a little odd."

His eyes were flat and unreadable when he glanced at her, then looked back out the windshield. "Something came up at work. I'm sorry if I seem preoccupied." She could see him relaxing his fingers on the wheel, but his shoulders and neck were still tight with tension.

Nick stared out the windshield, forcing himself to relax. *You almost had me convinced, lady. I was almost suckered into thinking you were on the level.* He glanced at Tess and his mouth thinned. *Yeah, you had me going.*

Jim's words still burned in his ears and echoed in his mind. "... a track sensation in college. Broke just about every record in the longer distances. One of the articles touted her as a sure bet for the next Olympic team." Jim had gone on to tell him that Tess had attended an exclusive eastern college whose track coach had described her as a "natural," the kind of runner who was born, not made. "After college, she dropped out of sight, apparently never ran any more races."

Nick snuck a glance at Tess and felt the rage building all over again. His jaw clenched as he thought about her wide eyed talk of being a private person and not wanting her life exposed for everyone to read about it. The traffic light ahead turned yellow, and he deliberately stamped down on the accelerator and shot through the intersection. Yeah, he just bet she didn't want her life exposed. Someone might find out the truth.

Glancing over at her again, he saw the silk of her hair hanging down her back. His body's instantaneous response just added fuel to his anger. *Brace yourself, Ms. Innocence*, he said to himself savagely. *You've got one hot reporter on your tail.* He'd get to the truth in the next five days, he vowed. He'd dig up every marathon she'd ever run in and spell out the details in his column. Once she was exposed for the little liar she was, how many companies would want her to endorse their products? The thought made his lips curve in satisfaction.

That must be some problem he had at work, Tess thought to herself. They were almost at the Greener Earth, and he hadn't said one word to her. He'd just sat there staring grimly out the windshield, acting like he wanted to hit someone. This was good, she tried to tell herself. If he was worrying about something at work, he wasn't thinking about her. An hour or two of her time talking about her running and she would be free to enjoy the rest of her Saturday in peace. She could hardly wait to do her laundry and watch those Hee Haw reruns.

Nick watched her out of the corner of his eye as he pulled into the yard at the Greener Earth. She leaned forward a little, scanning the area. In spite of his anger at her, he grudgingly admitted that she did seem to care about her business. The business itself was important, but he knew now that the idea the Greener Earth stood for was what really mattered to her. How could a woman with such strong ideals be so dishonest? The question bothered him, gnawing away at his subconscious. He'd try to figure that out after this assignment was over. Right now he'd better lighten up, or she'd realize he was on to her. He'd get more out of her if she still thought she had him fooled.

As they got out of the car, Nick called over, "How long do you think it'll take you?"

Tess looked over at him. He seemed to have forgotten whatever it was that had been bothering him. "I don't know for sure, but not too long. I'm just going to check the mail, make sure there's nothing urgent."

"I'll go check the bins for you."

91

He walked away, and Tess watched him for a moment. Shrugging her shoulders at his sudden change of mood, she walked in the door.

Five minutes later, she stared down at a piece of paper, her face white. "It's impossible," she whispered to herself. She grabbed her calculator and added up the numbers again. The answer was the same. Despair lodged like a fist in the back of her throat, making it impossible to swallow.

She knew they had collected more than this last month. They'd had to empty the bins every three or four days, so why was their total tonnage of material less than it had been the month before? She had been counting on this check to pay some of their more urgent bills. Now they would be lucky if they made payroll.

Hot, helpless tears welled up. The numbers in front of her grew blurry, then washed away altogether as her eyes filled. One by one the scalding tears dropped onto the receipt in front of her. She had to try to think of a solution, think of a way to get the money, but right now all she could do was stare at the piece of paper that spelled the end of her dream.

The door rasped as it opened and Tess stiffened. She had forgotten all about Nick. Quickly she wiped the back of her hand across her face. Maybe it wouldn't make any difference now if he found out about their problems, but he wasn't going to catch her crying about it, she thought fiercely.

"Tess? What's wrong?"

He sounded so concerned that she nearly started crying again. Praying that her voice would be steady, she answered, "Nothing except the usual bills." Pretending to be studying the papers on her desk, she added, "You know how it is with a small business. Nothing but problems the first couple of years." She hoped her voice was as light as her words.

Tess stared at her desk, acting like she was absorbed in her work until she heard him pick up a magazine and start to thumb through it. Glancing over at him, she quickly jumped up and hurried to the washroom. Leaning against the door, she looked at herself in the mirror. The blotchy, red face and puffy eyes definitely had to go before she could face Nick again. She stared at herself for a moment longer, then leaned over and started splashing cold water on her face.

When he heard the water running in the washroom, Nick stood up and walked over to Tess's desk. Even though she hadn't looked at him since he'd walked in the door, he knew she'd been crying. She had been in a good enough mood when he picked her up, so something must have happened while she was going through the mail.

He hesitated as he stood at her desk. The water was still running in the washroom, so he knew Tess wouldn't walk in on him, but the idea of rummaging around in her desk made him uncomfortable. He tried to tell himself that she had lied to him, so all bets were off, but somehow that didn't make him feel any better. Finally, reminding himself he had a job to do, he picked up the paper she'd been so absorbed in.

His heart twisted as he stared at the spots her tears had left. In spite of everything he'd found out, he suddenly wanted to tear open the bathroom door and cradle her in his arms. Looking at the tear-stained paper, her deception suddenly didn't seem so important.

An icy fist punched him in the gut, and he shook his head. No way was he going to be suckered like that again. Repeating to himself Jim's words of the night before, he looked down at the paper again.

As far as he could tell, it was a statement detailing how much glass and aluminum they had sold the previous month. The figure looked respectable enough, but he had no idea how much it cost them to operate the Greener Earth. Judging from Tess's reaction, he suspected it was a whole lot more than this.

Realizing that Tess had turned the water off, he

dropped the sheet of paper back onto her desk and slid into his chair. He just picked up his magazine when she walked out the door. There was no trace of tears on her face, even though she looked more pale than usual.

"Ready to go?" he asked casually.

She nodded. "I'm all set."

They walked in silence back to his car, and Tess settled into the passenger seat again, staring blindly out the window. She barely noticed Nick get into the car and start the engine.

"Tess?"

Nick's voice jerked her back to the present. Forget about this for now, she warned herself. It took every bit of willpower she possessed, but she turned to him with a smile. "Where to now?"

He looked at her for a moment, as if he wanted to say something else, then smiled back and said lightly, "How does a picnic sound?"

The smile spread to her eyes. "Somehow, you just don't seem like the picnic type."

His eyes glittered as he watched her. "I have all kinds of surprises up my sleeve."

Their eyes locked. The blue depths of Nick's eyes were as frigid as the deep ocean. He wasn't just talking about picnics, and Tess shivered. Then he blinked and smiled again, that lazy, crooked smile, and she wondered why she had been afraid.

"Well, let's see what kind of picnic you can conjure up from those sleeves of yours."

\*\*\*

"I didn't know you could have a picnic here." Tess looked around at the dense bushes that shielded them on three sides, leaving only the lake in front of them open to their view. "I could swear I saw a sign when we drove in that said no picnicking on the grounds."

Nick leaned back on the blanket, his long legs stretching out in front of him. Reaching into the basket, he pulled out a piece of cold chicken and grinned lazily at her. "I'm not sure what sign that was, Tess, but it sure looks to me like we're sitting here having a picnic."

"I guess I can't argue with that," she answered, swallowing a mouthful of chicken. "How did you ever find this little hideaway, anyhow?"

"I discovered it accidentally a few years ago. I was walking down that hill," he gestured toward the hill that rose behind the bushes, "when I slipped and started rolling. By the time I got to the bushes, I'd worked up enough momentum that I crashed right through." He chuckled and looked around. "It comes in handy for illicit picnics."

Tess had to laugh. They were in the middle of the Morton Arboretum, a two thousand acre tract of trees, meadows, and lakes. The trees were at the height of their fall color, and the Arboretum was jammed with people. She'd thought when they drove in that it was an odd place to choose for a picnic and interview, but tucked away on the far side of one of the lakes, they hadn't seen or heard a soul. "I'll say this for you, Bartholomew, you do have style."

Watching a family of geese on the lake in front of her, she didn't see Nick setting up his tape recorder until she heard the click as he turned it on. Instinctively she tensed, then slowly relaxed. They were going to talk about running today. There wasn't anything she had to hide, nothing she had to protect. She might actually enjoy this part of the interview.

"How long have you been running, Tess?" His voice was clipped and abrupt, a sharp contrast to the relaxed drawl of a minute ago.

"Well, I started training for the marathon about a year ago," she began, but he interrupted her.

"No, I mean when did you first start to run?"

Her eyes laughed at him. "If you believe my uncle, before I started to walk. According to him, I only had two speeds when I was a kid, stopped and full gallop." She leaned back and sipped her soft drink. "I was always fast, and when I got to high school I tried out for the track team. I did okay there, but when I went to college and started running the longer distances, I found my true love."

"What college did you go to?" His voice was casual as he looked out over the lake.

The Ivy League college didn't seem to surprise him, and she wondered suddenly if he'd already known the answer. Probably so, she thought. It must be standard procedure to research the person you're supposed to interview.

"Tell me about your college track experiences."

Was it her imagination, or was he suddenly less relaxed, more alert on the blanket beside her? "Well," she began slowly, "I ran a lot of different events, but I guess you could say my specialty was the five thousand and ten thousand meter races." She paused, unsure of how much he wanted to know.

"That doesn't tell me very much. Were you any good?" His voice was almost challenging.

Tess stared at him for a moment, then said drily, "I hold the conference records in both events. Do you really need to know all the details of my college races?"

Raising his eyebrows, he murmured, "No, I think I've got the picture. What about after college?"

She reached into the picnic basket, looking for an apple. Looking up at Nick again, she said quietly, "After college, I was ... burned out, I guess. I'd run in too many events, too often, and it wasn't fun anymore. I didn't run at all until I started to train for the marathon a year ago."

His eyebrows snapped together. "You're trying to tell me that you didn't run at all for four years and you prepared for and won the Chicago Marathon in a year?"

he asked incredulously.

"It's not that big a deal, you know." She shrugged. "It took me a couple of months to get back into running shape, then I had ten months to train for the race."

"And you didn't run any other marathons during that year?" He sat perfectly still, watching her closely, his eyes unreadable.

Her eyes were clear and open as she looked at him and shook her head. "I ran the marathon distance several times while I was training, of course, but never in an actual event." She gave him a puzzled frown. "But you know that from the interview at the race. I must have answered that question three different times."

"It's quite a feat, Tess, to beat all those world class women runners the first time you run a marathon. People want to know how you did it."

"I did it by working my rear end off, that's how I did it," she flashed at him. "I ran a hundred miles a week, sometimes more, for the last six months." She stopped and forced herself to calm down. "It's just a talent, Nick," she tried to explain. "Some people can sing, some can dance, and I can run. My coach in college told me I could do just about anything I wanted to do; he said I was a natural, whatever that's supposed to mean." She shrugged. "I trained harder than I ever did in college, and then just ran my race."

She paused, glancing out at the water then back at Nick. "I didn't have anything to lose, you see. I wasn't defending a title, or going for a world's record, or even trying to live up to the sportswriters' expectations. All I had to do was run fast." The corners of her mouth quirked upward. "That's the easy part for me. What's tough is when everybody expects you to win."

Nick watched her carefully. "What's up next?"

"Are you asking me if I plan to run in any more races?"

"That would be the logical question to ask the person who's just won the Chicago Marathon," he answered drily.

Tess laid back, folded her arms behind her head, and looked up at the sky. "I don't know what I'm going to do. The only thing I know for certain is that I'm going to keep running, because I enjoy it again. As far as any more races," she looked at Nick and shrugged again, "I haven't made up my mind."

Incredulous, he said, "Professional athletes make a lot of money, you know. Are you trying to tell me that you don't care about that?"

"I'd be a fool if I did, wouldn't I? Especially now that ..." She clamped her mouth shut, horrified by what she'd almost blurted out. Choosing her words carefully, she continued, "It's not that I don't care about the money, I just care about other things more. What would happen to my business, for instance, if I decided to take off every weekend to run another race?"

Nick's eyes narrowed as he looked at her. "You have a partner," he pointed out, watching her closely. "Can't he run things by himself?"

Still staring up at the clouds drifting high overhead, she murmured, "That's not the issue."

She sat up suddenly and faced him. Nick was lounging back on the blanket, his long legs stretched out in front of him, supporting himself on one elbow. He looked relaxed and nonchalant, but Tess wasn't fooled. Those intense eyes of his didn't miss much, and she wasn't foolish enough to think that he wasn't watching her carefully. It was time to change the subject. "What else did you want to ask me?" Her eyes dared him to ask about the recycling center again.

He stared at her for a moment, then leaned back, his lips twitching. "Why don't you tell me how you trained for the marathon?"

Crossing her legs Indian-style, Tess leaned forward eagerly. Her braid slipped over one shoulder, and she absently flipped it back. "It's all a matter of preparing yourself mentally," she began. She described how she'd gradually increased the number of miles she ran every day, then worked on increasing her speed. "By three weeks before the marathon, I knew that I'd be able to finish the race, but I wasn't sure how fast I could go. I was as surprised as everyone else when I won."

"Are you trying to tell me that you had no idea you were the first woman until you saw the finish line?" Nick demanded. "I can't believe that someone along the route didn't yell that out to you."

"They probably did," she admitted cheerfully, "but I didn't hear a thing. The only sound that got through to me was the background noise, the constant cheering and shouting. I was concentrating so hard on what I was doing that I wouldn't have noticed if my best friend had yelled at me."

Nick switched off the tape recorder. "Well, Tess, that's quite a story. It's going to make a real interesting column."

She narrowed her eyes. Something in his voice made her wonder just exactly what that column was going to say. Before she could pursue it, though, Nick sat up and took her hands.

"Tess, what's going on with your recycling center?" he asked in a soft voice, totally unlike the clipped tones of a moment ago.

She opened her mouth to tell him in no uncertain terms that the Greener Earth was none of his business, when he put his finger on her lips. "I'm not recording this, and I'm not writing it down. I know something is wrong. I heard what Mike said a couple of days ago and I could tell you were crying today when we were at the office. Maybe there's some way I could help you."

"I don't think anything could help," she said bitterly. Hesitating, she studied him. She longed with her whole heart to be able to trust Nick. It would be wonderful, she admitted, to be able to talk to someone about the problems they were having. Maybe someone who wasn't so involved with the recycling center could be more objective about it. What difference did it make now, anyway, she thought bitterly. She didn't see any way they could stay open for more than another month.

Seeing her hesitation, he continued gently, "Maybe it would help just to talk about it."

It was so tempting to give in. She didn't want to analyze why the urge to trust him was so strong. "Nick," she said slowly, "can you promise that nothing I tell you about the center will end up in one of your columns? Do you swear that this is just between you and me?"

He leaned forward and ran his knuckles down her cheek. "I can't promise you that the Greener Earth will never be mentioned in my columns. Where you work and what you do is part of who you are, and it's got to be part of my story. But if there's a problem and you want to keep it quiet, then I promise I won't mention it."

She stared at him for a moment, still hesitant to confide in him. She'd been successful so far in keeping their secrets, and it was difficult now to just blurt out the truth. Still, when Nick promised that he wouldn't write about their problems, she believed him completely. If he gave his word, he would keep it; she was sure of that. Besides, she wanted so badly to trust him. Telling herself again that next month there probably wouldn't be a recycling center to protect anyway, she sighed and looked down at the blanket.

"The Greener Earth has been losing money for the past several months. Lots of money," she stated baldly. "This morning I got a statement from the company that buys the material we collect. I thought we'd collected a lot more last month than we apparently had, and I was counting on some money that won't be there now. Anyway, to make a long story short, we're in big trouble."

Nick sat up, a puzzled frown on his face. "What about the money you won from the race? Fifty thousand dollars could certainly make a dent in your bills."

"It could and it already did." A smile flitted across

Tess's face. "The bank was getting a little anxious about the money we borrowed for the trucks. They were delighted that we were able to get our payments up to date, but there wasn't much left over after that."

"Why exactly are you losing money?" Nick ran his hand through his hair and leaned forward. "Where's the money going?"

"The problem doesn't seem to be that we're losing money," Tess answered slowly. "It seems to be that we're not making enough of it." Her lips curved at Nick's expression. "Yes, there is a difference. Our expenses are about the same, but our income seems to have dropped off lately. I'm not sure if people aren't putting as much out to recycle, or aren't bringing as much in to the center, but our total tonnage of material each month is way down."

"Are you sure that the company that buys the stuff from you isn't cheating you?"

Tess shook her head. "I don't think so. One of us always watches all the material being weighed, and we try to have a different person do it every month. I don't see how the company could cheat us."

"What are you going to do?"

She stared out at the lake, not looking at Nick. "I don't know. But until we decide, we don't want anybody to know we're having problems. If we could pick up even one more suburb as a client, we might be able to squeeze by. The problem is, if the people we're negotiating with find out that we're in trouble, they won't even consider signing a contract."

She looked back at him then. "That's why I didn't want you to know anything about where I work or what I do. I was afraid you'd find out we were in trouble, and I wouldn't be able to stop you from publicizing it."

"I gave you my word, Tess, and I'll keep it," Nick answered in a low voice.

"I know," she said softly. "I wouldn't have told you if I hadn't thought I could trust you."

Something twisted in his guts at her words. He recalled Jim's words the night before, and remembered the last time he'd trusted a woman. Well, this one had all the right words, but he was damn sure there was more to her story than she was telling.

He'd get to the truth if it killed him. He wasn't about to let a little thing like being attracted to the person he was interviewing stop him from doing his job. Gathering up the remains of their lunch, he shoved it into the basket and stood up.

"You about ready?"

By the time Tess stood up, he was already halfway through the bushes, waiting impatiently for her. Shrugging her shoulders, she followed him through the dense foliage. When the last bush had snapped back into place, he started up the hill without glancing at her. After a moment, Tess slowly followed him.

\*\*\*

Slouching on the couch, her head resting against the back, Tess listened to Nick's car pulling out of her driveway. The sound got fainter and fainter until it finally disappeared altogether. She still couldn't believe she'd actually told him about their problems at the Greener Earth.

It wasn't as if she didn't trust him not to write about what was going on. If he said he wouldn't, he wouldn't. She was certain of that. What was bothering her was the fact that she had confided in him so readily. Deep down, she knew why she had, and it scared her to death.

She was falling in love with him. The barriers she'd erected around her heart long ago were beginning to fall. She'd vowed that no one would be able to get close to her and then hurt her again like her uncle had, but somehow Nick had managed to worm his way into her soul. The thought was both exhilarating and terrifying at the same time.

She paced restlessly around the living room, then walked outside to sit on her back porch. Resting her elbows on her knees, she cupped her chin in her hands and stared, unseeing, into her yard.

Four more days. That was when her contract with the Chicago Post would be up. The promise in Nick's eyes when he told her that they'd talk in five days made her shiver all over again as she remembered. She had four more days to sort through her feelings and gather her courage. Then there would be no barriers between her and Nick. The next four days were going to be both the longest and shortest four days of her life.

# CHAPTER SEVEN

Nick laid his hands on his keyboard, hesitated, then began to pound out a staccato rhythm. His fingers flew as they tried to keep up with the words and sentences taking shape in his mind. Every time he felt himself slowing down, he glanced at the picture propped up on his desk next to his computer, and a fresh wave of anger propelled him along.

He'd found the picture earlier in the evening, while searching through endless pieces of microfilm on track events. The photograph of a younger Tess, holding up a trophy and smiling happily at the photographer, had jumped out at him. So had the man standing next to her, his arm draped around her shoulders. He'd recognized the man immediately, and as he stared at the picture he'd felt the floor crumbling beneath his feet.

Donald Phillips, entrepreneur of the decade, the man who'd found a million new uses for plastic, stared back at him proudly, his arm around his niece. Tess had just won an invitational track meet during her sophomore year in college, and the picture had found its way into the Chicago Post.

Nick stopped typing and picked up the picture. The now familiar pain throbbed dully in his chest as he looked at it once again. Until he found the picture, he'd tried to convince himself that all the flaws in Tess's story could be explained away. As angry as he'd been when he found out about her college track record, he'd still, deep down, hoped that she could explain why she'd kept it a secret. Now, staring at the picture of Tess and her wealthy uncle, he wondered if there were any kernels of truth in the things she'd told him.

It shouldn't hurt so much, he kept telling himself. He had suspected she was up to something from the very first, and he should feel triumphant right now. He certainly shouldn't feel like the brightness had disappeared from his life, leaving him with only the dull gray outlines of an existence. With a combination of pain and rage, he stood the picture up next to his computer and stared at the words on his screen without really seeing them.

What else could he think except that she was using him to get publicity? She certainly couldn't need the money she won in the marathon to pay her bills. And since that was her reason for submitting to an interview that she claimed was distasteful to her, he had to think that everything else she'd told him had been a lie, too. His temper boiled over again and he slammed an empty soft drink can into the wastebasket two feet away. We'll see how she likes the publicity she'll get tomorrow, he thought grimly as he began typing again.

\*\*\*

Tess smelled fresh coffee as she stepped out of the shower, and inhaled deeply. Her legs were pleasantly sore from her long run this morning, her body relaxed from her shower, and the coffee was ready. What more could you ask of a Sunday morning?

A fat Sunday Post, she thought happily a few minutes later, was the only missing ingredient. She'd dressed quickly and opened her front door to retrieve her paper before settling back with coffee and a croissant. Making herself comfortable, she scanned the front page headlines and started reading one of the articles.

Thirty minutes later, the coffee rose in her throat with the bitter taste of bile and the croissant sat in her stomach like a stone. She stared at the sports page in horror, unable to believe what she was reading.

Nick's picture had jumped out at her as soon as she'd looked at the sports section, and with great interest she had started reading his column. She hadn't gotten further than the first sentence when she started to feel sick to her stomach. Now, her hand was shaking so much that she had to put her coffee cup on the table to keep from spilling it.

"Why didn't he warn me?" she whispered. He hadn't even told her that the column was going to be about her, let alone what it was going to say. No, *imply*, she corrected bitterly. He had been as good as his word, not once saying directly that the Greener Earth was having problems. You didn't have to say anything directly if you were as good as Nick Bartholomew at hinting and insinuating.

Tess finished the column and sat staring at the page, trembling and sick. How could Nick have written these words? This was a man she thought she loved. Her stomach began roiling again as she thought back to the day before.

After they'd left the Arboretum, neither of them had been very talkative. She'd been relaxed, confident that Nick would be as good as his word and keep her secret. She'd even managed to convince herself that telling him herself was a smart move, because she'd been able to make him promise not to write about their problems. If he'd found out by himself, she wouldn't have had any leverage over him.

As they pulled up to her house she looked at Nick, uncertain. Now that there was no secret to protect, a solitary Saturday didn't seem as attractive. Clearing her throat, she said, "Do you want, I mean, would you like to come in for a while?"

Shaking his head, he avoided looking directly at her. He glanced her way then looked out the windshield again. "Sorry, I have some work I need to do today."

She'd quickly jumped out of the car. "Okay, I guess I'll see you on Monday, then." The car door had barely closed when the car roared off. Figuring that he'd been thinking about whatever it was he had to do, she shrugged her shoulders and walked into the house.

Now she realized why he'd been in such a hurry to leave. If this was what he really thought, he certainly wouldn't be interested in spending any spare time with her. Like a child with a scab who can't resist picking at it until it bleeds, she scanned over the column again.

"Why has Tess Phillips been so hesitant to speak to the press? Her story, if it's true, is a remarkable one. Why doesn't she want it told?"

Her teeth clenched as she reread the words, and anger slowly replaced the sick feeling. She had actually thought that Nick cared about her, that he wouldn't hurt her. Some judge of character she was, she thought bitterly.

Thinking about the way she had responded to his kisses, she cringed. He must have thought she was pathetic, trusting him so readily. Well, she had certainly made his job easier for him. She bet he'd had a good laugh over that.

She couldn't stop herself from looking at the column once again. "She seems to be sincerely committed to her business, the Greener Earth Recycling Center in Oak Ridge. In fact, most of her energy appears to be devoted to it. I think Tess herself wouldn't deny that it's the most important thing in her life."

What's he implying, she thought suddenly. Scanning down the column, she found another line. "After spending several days with Ms. Phillips, my question still is, how did Tess Phillips win the Chicago Marathon?"

She slowly straightened up. "He's trying to say that I

cheated somehow to win that race," she said incredulously. Quickly she scanned the rest of the column again. Here was another one. "A feat like this is almost unimaginable. A woman who never competed in a marathon before, didn't train with a coach, and had no real training regimen except just running, defeated five of the best women competing in world class marathons. I repeat, how did you do it, Ms. Phillips?"

Tess just stared at the paper in her hands. She couldn't believe her eyes. Never once had he even hinted to her that he didn't believe her story. He had questioned her pretty closely about her college track experiences, but she had figured that was just background information that filled out the story. "What possible reason could he have for not believing me?" she whispered.

At least he hadn't mentioned the problems with the Greener Earth, not directly anyway. He hadn't broken his word on that. The hints were there, though, if you knew what was going on. "Ms. Phillips is devoted to her business. It's more than just a job to her, it's a crusade. She's extremely protective of the recycling center, and takes all of its problems very personally." Yes, the clues were there, if you were looking for them. The implication was clear. This woman cheated somehow to win the race because she needed money for her business.

She pressed a hand to her stomach as she suddenly felt queasy again. Nobody else could possibly believe him, she tried to tell herself. The old saying about "where there's smoke, there's fire" flashed through her mind, and she felt another wave of nausea.

People believed what they read in the paper, especially when it came to sleazy innuendos. It wouldn't matter that none of the officials from the marathon had questioned her victory, or that nobody else had even suggested that she had cheated. If they read this in the newspaper, they would always wonder about her.

Standing up, she moved blindly away from the table,

bumping into the corner of the kitchen counter as she passed it. Barely glancing at the reddening bruise, she stumbled through the door into the living room and fell onto the couch. She shivered suddenly and pulled one of the afghans around her shoulders.

Nick. His face flashed into her mind, looking at her with his crooked grin. Oh God, was that all there really was to him, a handsome face and a great body? Did all that charm hide the fact that he had no soul? She shuddered again. If he could write a column like this about her, she thought, he definitely was lacking a heart.

Tess leaned back against the couch and closed her eyes. The fact that she had fallen in love with him certainly didn't say much for her judgment, she thought with a wince. But then, her track record in personal relationships was nothing to brag about, she reminded herself bitterly. She hadn't even spoken to her uncle in two years. The day she had told him she was quitting her job at his company to start the Greener Earth was the last time she had seen him.

She could still recall with perfect clarity the scene in his office that day. Her uncle had explained very calmly why she couldn't quit, especially to start something like a recycling center. It would make him look bad, he had said simply; make it look like his company was doing something wrong. As the niece of the owner and one of several vice presidents, she had a responsibility to the company that included not tarnishing its image. If she quit her job to start a recycling center, it would be nothing less than a slap in the face to the company and to him personally.

Tess had left his office half an hour later, white-faced and trembling. She hadn't seen her uncle since, and even though she told herself it was his choice, whenever she thought about him she was consumed with guilt. If she couldn't even maintain a relationship with her uncle, the man who had raised her, she thought wearily, why was she surprised that she had fallen in love with someone who despised her?

The sudden jangle of the telephone made her jump. She reached out to answer it, then paused. What if it was Nick? As soon as the thought entered her mind, she shook her head. No way would Nick be calling her this morning.

"Tess, please tell me you haven't read the newspaper yet," Donna's voice pleaded into her ear. "You just got back from your run, right?" she added hopefully.

"Sorry, you're about fifteen minutes too late," Tess answered lightly. It took every bit of control she possessed.

"I guess that means you've read that snake's column, doesn't it?"

"Well, it was hard to miss with his face plastered all over the sports page." In spite of herself, her voice wavered slightly.

"Paul and I will be right there," Donna said, speaking rapidly. "Three minds are so much better than one for plotting revenge. Don't mix any poisons without us." Without giving Tess a chance to answer, she disconnected the phone.

Tess stared bemusedly at the phone in her hand. Smiling slightly, she replaced the receiver. Count on Donna to fly to her rescue. In spite of the fact that she spent most of her time with Paul, Tess knew she could depend on Donna if she needed her.

It seemed like only a few minutes later that she heard the car pull into the driveway. Her front door burst open and Donna came rushing in, followed more slowly by Paul. Without saying a word, Donna enveloped her in a hug. Tess held on tightly, grateful for her unquestioning support.

Donna finally broke away to say with a disgusted look on her face, "Didn't I tell you that guy was nothing but trouble?"

For the first time since she'd looked at the paper that morning, a genuine smile appeared on Tess's face. "Yeah, Donna, I remember your warnings real well," she answered drily. "Gorgeous hunk was the way you phrased it, if I recall correctly."

"It's the gorgeous ones that are always the most trouble," Donna pointed out logically. She turned to her fiance with a grin. "Right, Paul?"

The tall, solidly built man sitting in a chair winked at them and drawled, "That's what all my women say."

After Donna had thrown a pillow at him, she turned back to Tess, her face serious again. "Tess, why does Bartholomew think that you cheated to win that race?" she demanded.

"God only knows. He hardly even asked me anything about the marathon. In fact, come to think of it, he seemed more interested in my college races than in the Chicago Marathon."

"You know," Paul interrupted, "a lot of his columns are about scandals and frauds in the sports world. From what I've seen, this guy redefines the word cynic. As a matter of fact," Paul stared thoughtfully off into space, "if I recall correctly, there was a big deal a few years ago with some woman tennis player. He was dating her or engaged to her or something, and all of a sudden he wasn't. Ever since, he's been particularly rough on women athletes." He looked at Tess and shrugged his shoulders, adding, "For what that's worth."

The lump in Tess's chest expanded until it felt like it would crush her heart. "You think he assumed I was guilty and I never proved that I wasn't?"

Paul shrugged again. "I don't know, Tess, I don't know the guy. From what I've seen of his column, though, that sounds about right."

The colors of the afghan Tess had pulled around her blurred and swam in front of her as she stared at it, unblinking. The lump in her chest must be ice, she thought, because she was numb, unable to feel anything. She barely heard Donna speak to her.

"So what do you think?" She looked up as Donna asked a question. "Tess, have you heard anything I said?"

"Sorry, Donna." Her smile was a little awry. "I guess I didn't."

Donna slid over to give her another hug, but not before she could hide the anger in her usually laughing eyes. "We're going to nail that bastard if it's the last thing we do," Donna vowed.

"No, we're not." Donna leaned back and stared at Tess in surprise. "I just want him out of my life, Donna. I don't want to have to think about him again." She almost laughed at that. She would think of Nick Bartholomew every day for the rest of her life, but she didn't have to tell Donna that.

"You're not going to just let him get away with saying those things about you, are you?" Donna was incredulous.

"You can't prove a negative, Donna. There's no way I can prove that I didn't cheat. And since there's no way that Nick can prove I did cheat—because I didn't—the louder I protest, the more people are going to think there's something funny going on. The only thing a public battle is going to accomplish is to make people more suspicious that I'm trying to hide something."

"You're going to just ignore what he said?" Donna was so furious she squeaked.

The sight of Donna, beet red and bouncing on the couch brought a reluctant smile to Tess's face. "What else can I do? Realistically, I mean."

"She's right, Donna," Paul interjected. "If she starts to squawk about Bartholomew, it'll only make her look more guilty." He turned his palms outward and shrugged. "It stinks, but a dignified silence is her best defense."

"Don't tell me that you're going to let that pond scum just waltz in tomorrow morning and take up the interview where he left off?"

The lump in Tess's chest moved and began to splinter, sending shards of pain along her nerves. "No, I may not be able to defend myself against what he's already written, but I won't give him any more stories." She looked blindly down at the afghan again. "Nick Bartholomew's interview with me is over."

"What about that contract you signed, Tess?" Donna asked softly. "He's just the kind of bastard that would hold you to the letter of the law and insist on a full week's worth of interviews."

"Then I'll pay him back for the three days that he'll miss." She straightened and looked at Donna again. "I'm not going to talk to him again."

"Tess, that's," Donna figured quickly in her head, "almost twenty-two thousand dollars. Where are we going to get that kind of money?"

The automatic "we" made Tess reach over and take Donna's hand. "I don't know, but we'll think of something." She knew, but didn't want to tell Donna. She knew how her friend would react.

"Hey, we can't scrape together enough money to buy a new bin for the Greener Earth. How are we going to come up with major money like that?"

"Don't worry, Donna, I'll think of something," she answered evasively.

She should have known Donna better. "You're going to go to your uncle, aren't you?" she asked. She was squeaking again.

"It's my money, Donna. All he does is control it. I'm only asking for what is mine anyway."

"Crawling is more like it," Donna answered darkly. "I can't bear the thought of you having to ask him for anything after the way he treated you when you left Phillips Plastics."

"My uncle took my quitting very personally, you know that. After all, I'm his only heir and he had ... plans for me." She sighed. "That's just the way he is."

"I'm not going to let you do it." Donna was vehement.

"Do you have any other suggestions?" For the first time, anger crept into Tess's voice. "I may not want to ask my uncle, but I can't think of any other way. Given a choice between eating some crow for my uncle and swallowing my pride and honor for Nick, I think I prefer the taste of crow."

"Tess, if there was any other way ..." Donna began, but Tess interrupted her.

"If there was any other way, I'd be taking it. Believe me, Donna, I'm not looking forward to this at all, but I'll survive."

"You may survive, Tess, but I'm not so sure about Bartholomew," Donna said darkly. "There must be something we can do to even the score a little. It's just not fair that he can get away with garbage like this," she threw the newspaper onto the floor, "and we have to sit here and take it."

A reluctant smile passed over Tess's face. "Fair would be Nick Bartholomew dying a slow, lingering death," she agreed. "But since that's not going to happen, we're going to pay off the rest of the contract and tell him to kiss off. It may not be much, but it's the only satisfaction we're going to get."

After a few more suggestions from Donna about inventive ways to torture Nick, Tess finally managed to send her and Paul on their way. Leaning against the door, her smile slowly faded from her face. At least Donna had managed to cheer her up. That had been the last thing she'd expected that morning.

Walking back to the couch, she saw Nick's face grinning up at her from the newspaper that lay on the floor. Without thinking, she sent it flying across the room with the toe of her shoe. Now, if only she could put him out of her mind that easily.

Tess thought about visiting her uncle, and a small knot of dread began to form in her stomach. It wasn't just the fact that she hadn't seen him in two years. She could deal with that. It was the way she knew he would make her feel, like a six-year-old child that had disobeyed her daddy. With a sigh, Tess leaned back on the couch and rested her head on one of the pillows. It was shaping up to be one hell of a day.

\*\*\*

Nick stepped off the elevator and looked around the room. Even on weekends it hummed with activity, and today was no exception. Men and women hunched over phones, scribbling down stories while other reporters pounded on the keyboards of their computer terminals. Apparently there was a lot going on in the sports world on this particular Sunday afternoon.

He almost made it to his desk before Arnie's voice bellowed at him. "That you, Bartholomew? C'mere, I wanna talk to you."

With an exasperated sigh, Nick stuck his head inside the door to his editor's office. "What is it, Arnie? I've got some phone calls to make."

"I want you to tell me about your column in this morning's paper. What exactly was on your mind?"

"Come on, Arnie. You told me to interview Tess Phillips and that's what I'm doing. I figured that would be obvious, even to you."

"The only thing that's obvious to me," Arnie shouted, waving the sports page in front of him, "is that you think you're writing for one of the supermarket rags instead of the Chicago Post."

"What exactly is that supposed to mean?" Nick marched all the way into the office and slammed the door. "Maybe you could spell it out for me."

"You were supposed to nail this Phillips broad." Arnie's fingers, cigar still clamped between them, stabbed toward Nick as he spoke. "I want facts, Bartholomew, not

115

all this supposition and hinting. I want to know exactly what she did and how she did it." He sat back suddenly in his chair. "That is, if she was lying. Could it be possible that you were wrong?"

Nick scowled in answer and looked out the window at the skyline of downtown Chicago. "She's lying, all right. I just haven't been able to find out yet where she ran her other marathons. She was some superstar runner in college, so it's not like she had no previous experience." He turned back to face Arnie. "On top of that, her uncle is Donald Phillips of Phillips Plastics. So where does she get off telling me that she has to do this interview because she needs the money?"

"I dunno, Bartholomew, you tell me."

"The whole thing stinks, Arnie, and just because I haven't put all the pieces together yet doesn't mean I'm not right. Don't worry, I have three more days with her, and I'll get the answers."

"Glad to hear it, Bartholomew. Now, get out of here and get busy. Just make sure you're doing your thinking with your brain and not what's in your jeans."

"Now, what the hell do you mean by that crack?" Nick shouted.

Arnie's eyes beneath his bushy brows skewered him with a look. "You've got the hots for her. The way I have it figured, that means you dump on her first and ask questions later." His look turned to steel. "You damn well better be able to back up your talk with some facts."

Opening his mouth to tell Arnie off, he thought better of it and stalked out the door. Still scowling, he stormed over to his desk and threw himself into his chair. Papers covered its surface, columns and articles torn from other newspapers and scraps and sheets of paper and envelopes with names, phone numbers, or cryptic phrases scribbled on them.

Staring at the mess on his desk, Nick thought involuntarily of Tess's desk, always neat and tidy. That led him to think of Tess, and how she looked as she sat at her desk, her braid slipping over her shoulder as she bent over her papers.

With an oath, Nick pushed away from his desk and stomped angrily to the water cooler. He'd come here to try to nail down some answers about Tess Phillips, not moon over her. As soon as he got the rest of this interview over with, he assured himself, he could forget all about her. All he had to do was make a few phone calls, find out where she had run her other marathons, and he was home free.

He walked back to his desk and looked down at the chaos. Somewhere in that pile, he was certain, was the answer to his question. Then why was he so reluctant to sit down and begin? He was even more reluctant to analyze the answer to that question. Out of the corner of his eye, he glanced at the picture of Tess and her uncle that he'd left sitting next to his computer. His mouth hardening, he sat down and picked up the telephone.

# CHAPTER EIGHT

Tess inhaled deeply and glanced at the sky. The faint light was a dull gray that seemed to wash away all the colors, making everything look dingy and dark. She shivered slightly as the wind cut through her clothes. This was more like late October in Chicago. The sun, just rising over the horizon, was obscured almost completely behind the dark clouds. If she was lucky, the rain would hold off until she had finished her run.

Bending once more to loosen her muscles, she started down the street, mentally plotting her route and pace. She was almost at the corner when she saw him lounging against his car. For a moment, not sure she could believe what she saw, she simply stared. Then she forced herself to continue at the same steady pace. He may have had more nerve than any two other men, but he wasn't going to have the satisfaction of watching her retreat.

She stared straight ahead as she ran past him. Even without looking at him she felt every slight movement he made. When he moved away from his car and fell into step next to her, she faltered momentarily, then kept on going. She refused to give him the scene he was probably expecting. There was no way she was going to provide him with material for his next column.

" 'Morning, Tess," Nick said smoothly as he ran along

beside her.

Tess finally looked at him, incredulous. He was staring straight ahead, outwardly relaxed and serene. Yesterday's column could have been a figment of her imagination for all the concern he showed about her reaction.

Her heart pounded as the adrenaline began to flow. A wave of anger washed over her, and she had to clamp her teeth together to keep from exploding at Nick. She fumed for another mile in silence until an idea began to form in her mind.

A glance at her watch told her they had run only a couple of miles. She was running close to seven minute miles, fairly fast but nothing like the pace it would take to win a marathon. Up ahead was an intersection, and making her decision, Tess turned to the left. They passed a few scattered offices, empty and desolate at this early hour, and came to a forest preserve entrance. Without hesitating, Tess turned in.

The road curved around for miles along the small DuPage River, Tess knew. It was a beautiful place to run, but Tess generally avoided it because it was so deserted at this time of the morning. Today, it was perfect for her plans.

Half an hour later, Tess glanced at her watch again. They had run at least seven miles, probably closer to eight. Sneaking a glance at Nick, she could see that he was tiring. His hair was matted down with perspiration, and his breathing was raspy and ragged. Tess smiled grimly. It was time to teach Mr. Bartholomew a little lesson.

"Nick, I understand you had some questions you didn't feel you could ask me directly." When Nick looked over at her, a question in his eyes, she continued, "About the marathon. You know, how exactly I won it."

"Ah, Tess, I don't think we need to discuss that right now, do you? Maybe after we finish this run we could sit down ..."

"No, I think this is the perfect time to discuss it," she

interrupted. "Actually, what I had in mind was a little demonstration." She wheeled abruptly and started running in the opposite direction, turning around and running backward as she spoke. "You want to know how I won the marathon, Bartholomew? Keep an eye on me and I'll show you."

Turning around again, she started to run. The seven minute miles she and Nick had been doing now seemed like no more than a fast walk. She was running at least five minute miles, the pace that a man has to keep up for twenty six miles to win the marathon. The wind streamed past her face and her legs pumped furiously. She wouldn't be able to go quite that fast for twenty six miles, but she could maintain it for a long time, plenty long enough for her purposes.

"Tess, stop!" Nick's voice echoed through the trees. Glancing over her shoulder, she saw Nick had stopped in the middle of the road. She watched him for a moment, then turned and kept running. The sight of him standing in the road, hands on hips, staring at her as she sped away was all the encouragement she needed to keep up the pace. When she felt the first raindrops a couple of miles later, she almost laughed out loud.

***

Tess sat at her desk at the Greener Earth, doodling on a pad of paper in front of her. The stack of papers on her desk was hard to avoid, but she was giving it her best shot. Even though she was sure that the explanation for their steadily dropping income was hidden somewhere in the pile of documents, she couldn't force herself to begin studying them. For the first time since the Greener Earth opened two years ago, something was crowding business out of her mind.

Not something, *someone*, she corrected herself ruefully. She was a sad case, indeed, if the sight of a man who had betrayed her trust and played her for a fool could set her pulses pounding and her blood racing. But that was exactly what had happened, she admitted, when she'd seen Nick leaning against the side of his car this morning. Pitiful specimen that she was, she had wanted to throw herself into his arms even while trying to figure out how to dismember him.

A hearty slap on the back startled her out of her reverie. "Nice work, partner," a voice boomed in her ear.

Tess spun around to see Mike leaning over her chair, a wide grin on his face. "Thanks, Mike, but what exactly did I do?"

"Great publicity, Tess." Seeing the puzzled expression on her face, he said impatiently, "The column in the paper yesterday. You know, written by that reporter who's been hanging around here."

Tess stared at him, incredulous. She'd never thought of Mike as Mr. Sensitivity, but she expected at least a small glimmer of sympathy from him.

"Mike, are you sure you read that column?" she asked in amazement.

"Yeah, he must have mentioned the Greener Earth at last five or six times. I'll bet the phone doesn't stop ringing today."

"He was saying that I cheated somehow to win the marathon in order to get money for the Greener Earth, Mike." She spoke slowly and distinctly, staring at her partner in disbelief.

"Who cares what he was saying? The important thing was that he was talking about us. You know, no such thing as bad publicity, get our name in the paper, all that sort of thing. Keep it up, partner."

Tess stared at Mike's retreating back in utter incredulity. Was her partner really that callous? She knew he wasn't stupid, and that if he had read the column, he would have realized immediately what Nick was hinting. She shook her head. Maybe in some bizarre, convoluted way Mike was trying to cheer her up, pretending there was some positive side to that column. Whatever it was, she wasn't about to try to figure it out right now.

The door banged open just as Tess pulled the stack of records in front of her. Donna walked in, glanced around, and plopped herself on the corner of Tess's desk.

"How are you doing today?" she asked softly.

"If I can motivate myself to start working on these invoices, I'll be doing okay." She didn't meet Donna's eyes.

"That's not what I meant and you know it!" Exasperated, Donna slid down into a chair and threw her purse onto the floor. "Has that slimy son of a toad had the nerve to call you yet?"

Tess bent over her desk, pretending to be busy. "No, he hasn't called. He just showed up this morning at six o'clock outside my door and started to run with me."

"What!" Donna sat up in the chair. "You're kidding, aren't you?"

Tess shook her head, smiling slightly at her friend's reaction. "He acted like nothing was any different from the last time he saw me."

"That man has nerve he hasn't used yet," Donna answered indignantly. "I hope you set him straight."

"I think I made my position clear," Tess replied with a grin. Talking to Donna suddenly made her feel much better. There was nothing like a sympathetic ear when it belonged to a good friend. She described with relish how she'd run Nick out eight miles or so, then left him there while she sprinted off. "The picture of Nick Bartholomew, standing in the middle of nowhere watching me run away is one I'll always treasure," she informed Donna, chuckling at the memory.

"It serves that arrogant horse's ass right," Donna said vehemently. "I just wish you'd taken him out ten miles farther and really made him suffer."

Tess laughed. "I think he's going to suffer plenty as it

is. He looked like he was hurting even before I left him. I suspect it was a real long walk home for Mr. Bartholomew." She laughed again. "Especially in the rain."

When Donna finally left and sat down at her own desk, Tess turned back to her stack of invoices with a little more enthusiasm. Trust Donna to cheer her up, even on a day when she would have bet it was impossible. Determined now to figure out what was going wrong at the Greener Earth, she reached purposefully for her calculator.

Tess had been working for quite a while when she realized suddenly that the room had gotten very quiet. Looking up, her eyes met the dark blue gaze of Nick Bartholomew. He stood in the doorway, watching her. It seemed to Tess as if the whole office was holding its breath, waiting for her reaction.

"Get out," she rasped in a low voice. She let her gaze linger on Nick for a moment longer, then looked down at her papers and blindly punched numbers into her calculator. She didn't look up when Nick deliberately sat down in the chair next to her desk. "I said get out of my office."

"Want me to throw him out for you, Tess?" The voice belonged to Tony, the driver who had collected the trash with her and Nick last week.

"Nah," said another voice, belonging to one of the other drivers, "I'd rather watch Tess do it herself."

Tess spun around in her chair, and the muffled laughter stopped immediately. Everyone was suddenly busy, looking anywhere but at Tess and Nick. Slowly she turned and looked at Nick. "I don't know why you're here, but we have nothing to discuss."

She started to turn back to her desk, but Nick caught the arm of her chair and held it so that she faced him. "Are you forgetting our contract, Tess?"

Her hands were cold. It took all her willpower to keep from rubbing them together to warm them. Forcing herself to look at Nick, she said quietly, "The interview is over, Nick. You're not going to get any more columns out of me." Taking a check out of her pocket, she handed it to him. "I think this will cover the three days that are still left on the contract."

Nick looked at the numbers on the check, then looked back at Tess, staggered. "Where did this money come from, Tess?"

The frozen rock in Tess's chest began to melt, replaced by a welcome rush of anger. "That is none of your business. Any right you had to ask me that question was forfeited by that column in yesterday's paper. Now, take the money and get out of here."

Nick stood up as if to leave, then grabbed her hand and pulled her out of her chair. Towing her along behind him, he slammed open the door and stalked out into the yard, shoving the door shut behind them.

"Okay, Tess, you've had your fun; now, I want some answers. Let's start with where you got this money."

Pulling her hand from his grasp, she backed up a step and regarded him coolly. "The interview is over, and you have no right to ask me anything. The only answers you'll get are when you ask for directions out of here." His impersonal, accusing glare as he stared at her seemed to finally release all her rage and grief. Anger welled up inside her like a volcano, temporarily smothering her pain. "Damn you, Nick, I trusted you," she cried. "I told you things ..." She paused, her voice shaking. "Things I shouldn't have discussed with anyone except Mike," she continued more softly. "And then you turned around and used it in your column. How could you, Nick?"

She hadn't thought it was possible for his face to look any more grim, but she was wrong. When he grabbed her shoulders and shook her, his fingers were hard and cold.

"Don't you talk to me about trust, Tess. You had me convinced that everything you said was God's truth. Such an idealist," he sneered, "with your environmental concern and your little recycling center. If your business was losing so much money, why didn't Don boy bail you out?" When she went white, he smiled thinly and let go of her shoulders, practically pushing her away from him. "Didn't think I'd find out who your uncle was, did you?"

Her uncle. For a moment she almost laughed in his face. The scene in her uncle's study yesterday leaped into her mind. She could smell the leather book bindings, the lemon scent of the furniture polish. She saw her uncle leaning back in his chair, into a shaft of sunlight. His voice rang harshly in her ears. "So, Tess, when you need help with your little business you come crawling back to me. I suppose I should be flattered."

It had taken every bit of her resolve not to turn around and walk out of the room. "I'm only asking for what will be rightfully mine in a year anyway," she'd replied evenly. "You can think of it as a loan if you want to." Not for the first time, Tess cursed the terms of her parents' will that left her trust fund totally in her uncle's control until she turned twenty-six. In spite of the fact that with the money her uncle controlled she wouldn't have to worry about the Greener Earth's finances at all, she'd only come to her uncle as a last resort. She'd known what her reception would be.

Scowling, her uncle had pulled out the big, leather embossed checkbook and scribbled across a document. "Can't have a Phillips fail in business, can we?" he demanded. Handing her the check, he closed the checkbook with a quiet thud. "I certainly hope that's all you'll need."

That was the extent of his concern, she thought dismally. Not that she was all right, not that he could help her, but that she not disgrace the Phillips name and let her business fail. Well, wasn't that the way it had always been? Squaring her shoulders, she turned and walked out the door. The door was half shut when he spoke again, gruffly. "I watched your race on television. You did a good job, Tess." Not that he was proud of her, or that he wished he could have been there. Her tears didn't start falling until the door was closed.

Now, as she looked back at Nick, all the rage and anger disappeared, leaving only the grief. His eyes were still burning into her, accusing her of God knows what. All she knew was she had to get away from him. "Just take the money and go, Nick," she said in a low voice. She had turned and was walking back toward her office when he grabbed her from behind and spun her around.

"It's not quite that simple, Tess," he ground out. "This turned out to be more than just another column for me. Not only did I trust you, I actually thought I was in love with you." He sneered at her stunned expression. "Yeah, babe, I guess I should thank you for reinforcing a lesson I learned a long time ago. Don't get involved with a jock. They're the most deadly broads in the world."

She could only stare at him. Nick swore at her huge blue eyes that seemed to be swimming in pain. A dame who'd pulled a fast one on him like she had didn't have the right to look like the injured party. Before he could think about it, he pulled her into his arms.

He wanted to punish her, make her hurt like he had suffered the last two days. His lips were hard and demanding, not soft and tender like a lover's. He wanted to take from her, to try to recover all that she had taken from him. If his mouth and lips were hard enough, cold enough, maybe he could draw his heart back out of her hands.

His anger tasted bitter on her tongue. There was no gentleness to his kiss, no kindness. There was only his lips and teeth and mouth, hard, demanding, not asking of her. Mocking what he had just said to her, as if he was trying to convince himself it wasn't true. For just a moment, she tried to pull away, pushing at his chest with both hands. Then, with a suddenness that surprised even her, she collapsed against him. Cupping his face in her hands, she was returning his kiss with a fire that she didn't even recognize.

Her body was like a pile of dry tinder, and his lips were the match. She wrapped her arms around him to keep herself from sliding to the ground. Running her hands up and down the muscles of his back, she pressed him closer. All of her anger, all the grief had vanished, leaving only her need for him.

She wasn't sure when his kiss had changed. His mouth was still demanding, still hard, but now there was passion there instead of anger, desire instead of rage. When his tongue twined with hers, he gave as well as took. The hands which had grasped her shoulders now caressed her back and slid down to her hips. When he lifted his mouth from hers, it was to mutter her name.

They broke apart, both gasping for breath, Nick looking as shocked as she felt. Her blood was churning, her heart was pounding, and desire for him burned inside her. She took two steps backward, still staring at him, then turned and fled into the building. She didn't know that the despair she saw on his face mirrored the look in her eyes.

*\*\**

After she punched the same set of numbers into her calculator for the fourth time, Tess pushed the machine away from her with an oath and stood up. It had been twenty-four hours since Nick had stormed into the office, and she still couldn't concentrate on what she was doing. "I've got to get out of here for a while," she muttered to no one in particular. "I'll be back when ..." Turning around, she saw several pairs of sympathetic eyes watching her. It was just enough to upset the fragile hold she had on herself. She hurried out the door and into her car before the tears watering in her eyes could overflow.

The familiar patterns of the yard wavered and blurred in front of her as she sat behind the steering wheel.

Staring blindly out the window, she fumbled for a tissue from the box next to her.

Her recycling center, the project that had been her life for the last two years, had become a place too painful for her to work. It was as if the past two years had ceased to exist. Her only memories of the Greener Earth centered around Nick. When she was in the office, all she could see was his long form lounging in the easy chair, asking one of his endless questions. Out in the yard, she saw him lifting the lid of one of the bins, cheerfully calling out to her its status.

Tess blew her nose and wiped her eyes. She needed to run for a while. That always helped to clear her mind and blow away the cobwebs. Starting the car, she eased it slowly into gear and pulled away.

An hour later, she glanced over at the river and wondered how she had gotten this far. Her legs had been working automatically, letting her mind wander. Obviously it hadn't wandered too far, because this was the same route she had run with Nick just yesterday morning. Feeling a twinge in her knee, she slowed down a fraction. It was probably time to turn around and head back.

This was one problem that running wasn't going to be able to help her solve. She could run all day and all night and still not be able to put Nick Bartholomew out of her mind. If she ran until she was exhausted and then fell into bed, her dreams would be filled with his face.

She slowed to a walk, then stepped closer to the riverbank. Spotting a fallen log, she sat down and stared out over the quiet water. It already smelled like fall, the decaying leaves all around her filling the air with a rich earthy aroma. A few brown, curled oak leaves floated silently down the river. A cold front had come through, making the wind bite through her shirt. All Tess could see was Nick's face telling her he'd fallen in love with her. Telling her, all too clearly, that he considered it possibly the biggest mistake he'd ever made.

Women had fallen in love before and gotten over it, she tried to tell herself. The pain would be less tomorrow, then less the day after that. She just had to get through each day, one at a time, and each night. Her toe found a pebble and she kicked it into the water. That was all there was to it. She would just get on with her life. Instead of standing up and starting home, though, she just sat and stared at the slowly moving water. She never heard the low rumble of the sports car as it cruised slowly down the road, or the whine as it sped back in the other direction a little while later.

\*\*\*

Nick set his cup of coffee down on the stack of papers on his desk, sloshing some of the black liquid onto a pile of tattered-looking notes. Swearing, he grabbed a wad of paper out of the wastebasket and wiped it off, leaving a brown smear. As he picked up the top papers and waved them in the air to dry, he glimpsed a photograph underneath and once again the faces of Tess and her uncle stared up at him.

Feeling his already black mood worsen as he looked at the photo, he picked up the picture, wadded it into a ball and heaved it into the wastebasket. He turned back to his computer, but as he stared at the screen, he saw Tess's face instead of the blinking green lights.

The image of her face when he'd mentioned her uncle the day before had been lurking in his mind ever since their confrontation. He'd done his best to banish it, even going so far as to ask one of the secretaries from the office out last night. The evening had been a disaster, in spite of the fact that the secretary was well-endowed, cheerful, and more than willing to comfort him. Her bright chatter about fashion and the latest office gossip had only made her seem superficial and shallow next to Tess. He'd ended up dropping her off early and spending the rest of the evening trying to forget about Tess with the help of a bottle of twelve-year-old scotch.

The scotch hadn't helped, and now the sight of the picture had brought her face back in his memory all too vividly. He reached down into the wastebasket and retrieved the photo, carefully smoothing it out. The Tess of several years ago beamed up at him, apparently pleased with herself and happy that her uncle was standing at her side. It was a totally different picture than the one of Tess yesterday. At the mention of her uncle, she had looked as if he had slapped her.

Maybe, he thought slowly, her uncle was the key to understanding what was going on here. If he could find out what was between Tess and Donald Phillips, perhaps he could figure out all the answers to his other questions. He put his hand on the phone and hesitated while he tried to decide who to call first. He was just starting to punch the numbers when someone plopped down on his desk.

"Great column on Sunday, Nick." Jim Krieg, the young reporter whose desk sat across the aisle from his, was grinning at him. "I guess you put that Phillips woman in her place."

Nick scowled at him. "What the hell is that supposed to mean?"

"You had some great lines, I'll give you that," Jim said breezily. "So tell me," he raised his eyebrows, "how did she cheat in the Marathon?"

Nick pushed away from his desk and stalked over to the coffee machine. "I haven't found out yet what other marathons she's run in, but I'm working on it," he tossed over his shoulder.

"Come on, Bartholomew, you can tell me. You wouldn't write a column like that unless you had some proof, would you?"

Nick swore at the young reporter, not deceived by the innocent look on his face. "Knock it off, Krieg. You're beginning to sound like Arnie."

Jim stood up and strolled back to his desk. "Yep, you really outdid yourself this time, Bartholomew."

Nick frowned at him and looked back at his computer. "Damn young snot," he muttered. He shook his head, deciding to forget about Jim's not so subtle comments for the time being. Discovering the story behind Tess and her uncle was the only thing he wanted to think about right now.

Several hours later, he slowly set the phone receiver back in its cradle, more disturbed than he had been in a long time. He had just finished talking to Tess's college track coach, a man who had been extremely reluctant to talk about Tess Phillips and her relationship with her uncle, Donald. He remembered Tess very well, he'd said, and had been happy to tell Nick how many races she'd won in college and all the records she'd broken.

As soon as Nick had mentioned her uncle, though, the coach had clammed up. He'd suddenly been very busy, someone had just walked into his office, and could he get back to Nick? Nick stared at the phone, thinking. Something stunk, and he was going to find out what it was.

Suddenly he reached into a desk drawer and pulled out an address book. Thumbing through the pages, he finally found the entry he was looking for. With a smile of satisfaction, he dialed a phone number, then leaned back in his chair. He smugly congratulated himself for remembering the name of the sports editor of the newspaper in the small Massachusetts town where Tess had attended college.

A few minutes later he sat up in his chair, scribbling furiously on a piece of paper. "Are you sure about all this?" he asked incredulously. He listened as the editor assured him that it was common knowledge, everybody on the staff of the athletic department knowing what had happened.

"It was a disgrace, and the coach deserved to be fired," the voice on the other end of the telephone said emphatically. "Unfortunately, the head of the athletic department preferred to shut his eyes and just hold out his hand for the money. Nobody was interested in what that poor kid felt, not her coach, not the athletic director, not even her own uncle, who I understand had raised her. When the kid walked off the field in the middle of the N.C.A.A. championships, everyone in the press box cheered like crazy."

Nick's pencil flew across the page. "You're sure this is all verifiable?"

"Absolutely." The editor gave him several more names of reporters that worked for other newspapers or television stations in the area. "Any of those guys will tell you the same thing. That was what was so disgusting about the whole deal. Nobody went to any particular trouble to hide what was going on." The editor paused, then asked quietly, "I always wondered what happened to that kid. Did she ever run in another race?"

"She just won the Chicago Marathon," Nick answered slowly. "She says it's the first one she's ever run."

"I don't know about that, but she sure deserves it. I haven't ever, before or since her, seen anyone so talented. Or anyone, at least in the beginning, who loved to run as much as she did. That's what makes what they did to her so obscene. Tell her congratulations from me." He hung up, leaving Nick staring off into space before he carefully hung up the phone.

Nick looked down at the picture of Tess and her uncle again, and he felt the familiar anger burn his throat. This time, though, it wasn't aimed at Tess, it was for Donald Phillips.

According to the man he'd just talked to, Tess's college coach had entered her in too many events, too often, taking advantage of the superb natural athlete he was coaching in order to rack up victories for the college and glory for himself. Tess's uncle, according to the editor, had encouraged him, donating more money to the college's athletic fund each time Tess won an event.

The coach had ignored the requests from Tess to run in fewer events, telling her that in order to stay on the track team she had to be productive. When Tess walked off the field during the 10,000 meter race in the N.C.A.A. finals her junior year, her coach had been furious but couldn't convince her to return to the team. As far as the newspaperman knew, she hadn't set foot on a track since then.

Picking up his cup of coffee, Nick tasted the cold liquid and absently put the cup back down. He rubbed a hand over his eyes. All that scotch the night before had been a big mistake. He needed to get the cobwebs out of his brain, and this foul concoction they called coffee wasn't doing the job.

Everything Tess had told him agreed with what the editor of her college town paper had said, he admitted. She had left out large chunks of it, but what she'd told him had been true. The thought glimmered on the edge of his consciousness that maybe everything else she'd told him was true, too. He moved uneasily in his chair. Now, wouldn't that be a hell of a note, he thought sourly. He finally finds an honest athlete and he doesn't believe her story. Not to mention falling in love with her. Yeah, that would be poetic justice, all right.

Leaning back in his chair, he replayed the events of the last few days. Somewhere, he was certain, there was a clue that would tie everything together for him. Why did Tess need money if her uncle was one of the wealthiest men in the state? Why, if she was such a talented athlete, had she not competed for at least four years? *Why was she so determined to keep him at arm's length?*

He started to paw through the stack of papers on his desk once again, looking for a phone number he had carelessly scribbled on a scrap of paper a couple of days ago. Suddenly he stopped. He didn't want to talk to another source, he needed to talk to Tess herself. Pushing himself away from his desk, he hurried into the elevator.

\*\*\*

"She's not here."

"Ah, do you know where she is?" Nick asked cautiously.

"Sorry, I don't." The look in Donna's eyes said that she wasn't sorry at all, and that even if she knew where Tess was to be found, she wouldn't have told him to save his life.

"Well, if you talk to her, tell her I'm trying to get in touch with her."

Donna didn't even bother to answer this time, simply staring at him like he was a bug that had appeared in her salad. Nobody else in the Greener Earth's office looked very friendly either, for that matter. Nick looked at the hostile faces one last time, then turned around and walked out the door.

He drove over to her house, feeling hope surge within him when he saw her car in the driveway. After knocking on both doors and peering in several windows, though, he was forced to admit she wasn't there. Climbing back into his car, he slammed the door shut in frustration. As he drove slowly down the street, thinking idly how familiar it had become from his runs with Tess, he suddenly realized where she must be. Whenever she was upset, she ran. He pressed the accelerator, determined to cruise her usual routes until he found her.

The road along the river was his last hope. Sometime during the last hour, while he was driving up and down the streets where Tess usually ran, it had become vitally important that he find her. He had to try to erase the despair he'd seen in her eyes that morning, and until he understood why it was there, he didn't have a chance. He was sure she was out here somewhere running. And he was determined to find her.

He drove all the way to the end of the river road with no sign of her. Turning the car around, he pushed the accelerator closer and closer to the floor.

Maybe he'd missed her somehow, and she was at home already. By the time he rounded the big curve, he was traveling at almost sixty miles per hour. He didn't catch a glimpse of the figure sitting so quietly on the fallen log.

# CHAPTER NINE

Tess stared at the ringing phone, willing it to stop. This was the third time this evening its shrill sound had intruded into her living room. The first two times, she'd picked up the receiver and heard Nick's voice on the other end. Without even stopping to listen to his words, she'd gently laid the phone back in its cradle. This time, she promised, she wouldn't pick it up no matter how many times it rang.

It had been a week since the last confrontation with Nick at the Greener Earth. The phone calls had become a nightly ritual. Thank goodness, he had at least stopped coming to the recycling center. After the first two days, they had simply kept the door locked. She still wasn't able to get much work done while she was there, but at least she didn't have to worry about Nick suddenly appearing and plopping himself in the chair next to her desk.

The sound of a key in the front door made her realize that the phone had stopped ringing. When Donna stepped through the door, Tess smiled. If anyone could take her mind off Nick Bartholomew, it was Donna.

"Paul's working late and I didn't want to eat alone," she said easily. "Want some pizza?" She flourished the square box in front of her.

"Thanks, but I'm not hungry," Tess murmured. She

watched as Donna set the box on the table right in front of her. The smell of tomato sauce and melted cheese made her stomach rumble. Surrendering with a smile, she reached out for a piece of the hot pizza. "You really are underhanded. You know that, don't you?"

Grinning back, Donna peeled off her coat and replied, "Whatever it takes. The thought of you sitting here, moping by yourself, has been driving me crazy. The least I can do is mope with you for a while."

Donna settled back on the couch and helped herself to the pizza. "So, what's the latest word from our favorite reporter. Has he come to his senses yet?"

Shrugging her shoulders, Tess said, "I have no idea. I haven't talked to him since that day at the Greener Earth." She took another bite and added, "And I have no intention of talking to him again."

Donna cocked an eyebrow. "How can he grovel if you don't give him a chance?"

"He doesn't want to grovel. All he's interested in is where I got the money to pay him off."

"Hey, maybe you're wrong. The least you can do is give him a chance to explain."

"Whose side are you on, anyway?" Tess rose and walked into the kitchen, returning in a minute with two cans of beer. "Besides, I'm not interested in any explanations or apologies. I just want to forget all about him."

"Tess," Donna said gently, "it's time you stopped trying to insulate yourself from your feelings. It's not your fault that your uncle is a jerk. Nick has nothing to do with your relationship with him."

"Now, where in left field did that come from?" Tess stared at Donna in bewilderment.

"Come on, Tess," Donna said impatiently, "ever since you quit Phillips Plastics I've watched you retreating from your feelings. You figured if you got wrapped up enough in the Greener Earth you wouldn't have to deal with anything messy like emotions. Just because your uncle can't accept you for what you are doesn't mean that no one else can."

"I think you've finally gone around the bend. What on earth does my uncle or Phillips Plastics have to do with Nick?"

"You're trying to pretend that you don't give a damn about Nick, and it's not going to work. If you really loved him, you'd give him a chance to explain why he wrote that column. You just don't want to take a chance because you're afraid that he'll kick you again like your uncle did."

"I think Nick has already made his position on me perfectly clear," Tess murmured, without looking at Donna.

"Yeah, well, then why has he been so determined to see you?" Donna demanded.

Just then the phone rang again. Tess stared at it, praying that it would stop. It just rang on and on, each ring making her coil even tighter inside.

"Why don't you answer the phone, Tess?" Donna goaded. When she didn't get an answer, her smile was smug. "That's what I thought."

"Donna, how could he love me and write a column like that?" Tess whispered. "I feel so betrayed."

"The only way you're going to find out is by asking him." Donna spoke softly. "You can't just mope around here and say you're going to forget about him. At least confront him about it."

Remembering what had happened the last time she had confronted Nick made her flush a dark red. She could still remember with vivid clarity the feel of Nick's long, hard body pressed against her. If she closed her eyes, she could still taste his lips. The memory of the moment when anger had turned to desire was crystal clear in her mind.

Even now, thinking about it made her squirm with shame. It must have been a real kick for Nick to realize how much she still wanted him, even after what he had written.

"I can't, Donna; believe me, I just can't." She stood up and gazed out the window. It looked more like fall now, with the leaves almost gone from the trees and their bare branches ghostly in the light of the street lamp. They looked like she felt, barren and lifeless and cold. Without turning around, she said, "Thanks for coming over. I guess I'll see you at work tomorrow."

Donna walked over and gave her a hug. "I know when I'm getting the bum's rush. At least think about what I said, okay?" Without waiting for an answer, she shut the door quietly and was gone.

Tess watched until her taillights disappeared from view, then turned and walked slowly into her bedroom. The bright colors of the bedspread and curtains and the cheerful prints on the wall didn't improve her mood. Throwing herself down on the bed, she crossed her arms behind her head and stared up at the ceiling.

\*\*\*

Nick listened to the ringing telephone and swore under his breath. He knew she was there. He could feel her refusing to pick up the phone. Slamming the receiver back down, he stalked to the front of his apartment.

He stared out the window blindly, not seeing the bare branches of the oak trees bending in the wind. Dammit, why wouldn't she answer the phone? Running his fingers through his already unruly hair, he leaned his forehead against the cool pane of glass.

Every day that passed since he'd last talked to her only made him more determined to find out the truth. Ever since he'd talked to the editor of her college town newspaper, he'd known that there was a whole lot more to her story than she'd told him. By now, a week later, he'd become obsessed with the need to hear it from Tess herself. He tried to tell himself that it was just journalistic responsibility, the need to tell the whole story. But he knew, and sometimes would even admit, that there was more to it than that.

In spite of his vows to never get involved with an athlete again, he'd fallen in love with her. Even when he was sure she was lying to him, he still loved her. Now, when he was beginning to suspect that he was the one who had made a big mistake, he was almost frantic with the need to see her.

He hadn't found a trace, not even a hint, that Tess had ever run in another marathon. He'd spent a couple of days poring over the results of countless marathons in the area, and some that were quite a distance away from Chicago. Not only was her name never mentioned, the pictures he'd found of winners had most definitely not included Tess. He had been forced to admit that she must have been telling the truth when she said this was her first marathon.

He'd come to realize in the last few days that deep down, he'd probably known she was telling the truth all along. Wasn't that one of the things that had attracted him to her in the first place, her sincerity? If he hadn't been so damn sure that she had some angle, he probably would have seen it a long time ago.

He'd called himself every name he could think of this past week, but it hadn't made him feel any better. He needed to know where she'd gotten the money to pay off the contract. Still staring outside, he slowly realized that the logical place would be her uncle. Straightening up, he hurried back to the phone.

"Jim. Thank God, you're still at work. Do me a favor, will you, and get my address book out of my desk? Yeah, thanks." He waited impatiently while Jim Krieg rummaged through his desk drawer. "Okay, is there an entry for a Mike Angelos?" He scribbled the number down, thanked Jim again and hung up the phone.

Nick looked at the number for a moment, then picked up the phone again. Mike was a reporter for another newspaper in town. Nick had gotten to know him while they were both working on a story about business sponsorship of athletic teams. Phillips Plastics had come up in the conversation, and although Nick had forgotten the reason, he hoped that Mike would have more information on the company and its owner, Donald Phillips.

The seven rings that Nick counted seemed endless. Finally, just as he was about to give up, a breathless man answered the phone.

"This is Nick Bartholomew, Mike." They exchanged pleasantries for a minute, then Nick explained why he was calling. "Do you know anything about her relationship with her uncle?"

"What relationship?" Mike asked bluntly. "After she quit the company to start her recycling business, the bastard refused to have anything more to do with her."

"What?" Nick practically shouted into the phone.

There was a pause on the other end of the line, then Mike laughed softly. "She never told you about that, did she? Well, take it from me, it was a first class battle even though it was completely one-sided. When she told the old man she was leaving, he blew his stack, told her that if she left, she could forget about having anything to do with him. I have to give her credit, she stood up to him."

Nick sank back in a chair. "So she was actually working for him?"

"Hell, yes, she was one of his vice presidents. That's what galled him so much, or so I heard. He handed her the company on a silver platter, and she told him she couldn't work for a company that was so environmentally irresponsible. Like I said, the woman had some guts."

They talked for a few more minutes, then Mike asked, "How's her business doing, anyway?"

"Not so well, I'm afraid," Nick answered slowly. When Mike told him to keep in touch, he responded automatically, then hung up the phone.

Either Tess had some source of money that was a complete mystery to him, or she had gone back to her uncle to get the money to pay him off. Knowing what he did about Tess by now, he was sure it had been her uncle. He felt anger burn his throat as he thought about Tess having to ask her uncle for twenty-two thousand dollars. And she had done it, he thought with a sick feeling in his stomach, to avoid having to talk to him.

\*\*\*

The windshield wipers swept silently across the window as Tess peered out through the steadily falling rain. The storm that had been threatening for the past two days had finally broken, and the dark clouds, wind and cold rain were the perfect mirror of her mood. Driving home from the Greener Earth after another unproductive day, Tess was almost glad to see the rain. It was a good excuse for her dismal disposition.

The streets around her house were completely deserted. Even though it was only six o'clock, the darkness of the storm made it seem much later. Her headlights picked out a few cars parked along the curb, but no one was foolish enough to be outside this evening.

She had parked the car in her driveway and was half way to her front door when she noticed the man standing on the front porch. He huddled under the slight overhang of the roof, but he was clearly soaking wet. It didn't take more than a brief glance to tell her who it was.

Stopping on the lawn, she simply stared at him. Even though she'd known that she'd be forced to face Nick eventually, the last place she'd expected to see him was on her doorstep in weather like this. She was barely aware of the rain when he spoke.

"It's at least a little drier up here," he said gravely.

She took one more look at his face and turned around to walk back to her car. She hadn't gone more than two steps when he caught her wrist.

"I haven't stood out in this rain for an hour so that you can run away from me again. I want to talk to you, Tess."

"Well, I don't want to talk to you. I think everything that matters was said in your column." She tried to pull her arm away, but he tightened his grasp.

"Not quite, Tess." His voice was grim. "If you really want to do this out here in the rain, that's fine with me. I'm already soaked. The neighbors might appreciate the show, too. I'm not going to leave, though, until we've talked."

Panic fluttered in the back of Tess's throat. *Please, just go away*, her inner self pleaded. "Nick, I ..." she faltered as he watched her steadily. Seeing the determination in his eyes, she turned abruptly and walked up the stairs to the front door.

*You might as well get this over with*, she thought as she let him into the house. His phone calls every evening were beginning to drive her crazy, she told herself firmly, and this was the way to put a stop to them. Thinking about not hearing from Nick again did nothing to improve her mood.

She took off her soaking wet sweater and hung it in the closet, and watched Nick peel off his sweatshirt and drop it casually on the floor. Her silk blouse and cotton slacks were equally wet, and water was dripping from her braid down her back. Trying to ignore them, she turned to Nick.

"What exactly do you want?"

He looked at her for a moment, then without speaking he led her into the bathroom. Pulling the elastic band out of her braid, he unwound the soggy plaits and rubbed her hair vigorously with one of her towels. When he'd finished, he used the towel on his own hair, then calmly hung it back on the bar and waited for her to go back into the living room.

Bemused by the gesture, Tess walked slowly back to

stand in front of the couch. Facing him, she clenched her hands behind her back. It was ridiculous - that she should be so touched by such a small thing. Ridiculous or not, though, if she didn't get him out of here fast, she was really going to make a fool of herself.

"Why didn't you tell me about your uncle?"

The question was so unexpected that she sank onto the couch. "What do you mean?" she asked slowly, feeling dense.

Nick turned away from her to look out the window. "I think you know what I mean. How you used to work for your uncle, why and how you quit, why you haven't talked to him for two years." He turned back to look at her, and smiled grimly as he saw her flinch. "And especially what he did to you while you were in college. How he made sure you were completely burned out on running. Didn't you think that was relevant to the story, Tess?"

"No," she cried passionately. "That has nothing to do with the Chicago Marathon. That's my business, between me and my uncle. You had no right to go sniffing around in my personal life like that. Now, I suppose," she added bitterly, "that'll be the topic of your next column." She jumped up and strode around the room, stopping a few feet from Nick. "This is exactly why I didn't want to be interviewed. You'll drag all this up again, discuss my family business with excruciating detail, and tell the whole world about how my uncle and I don't get along."

"Do you really think I'd do that to you, Tess?" Nick asked quietly.

"After last week's column, I'd believe you could write just about anything about me."

He turned around. "The reason I wrote last week's column was precisely because you hadn't told me those things. When I found out who your uncle was, I went nuts. I figured you were hiding all sorts of things, including other marathons you must have run in. If you had told me all that stuff about your uncle, everything would have made more sense."

She sat, stunned, at the revelation. She'd spent a lot of time the past week trying to figure out exactly how he thought she had cheated. Having previous marathon experience and lying about it was one that had never even crossed her mind. Well, at least he'd suspected her of something original. "So the fact that you wrote that column full of insinuations and innuendos is entirely my fault." Her chin tilted slightly, in a challenging gesture.

"Damn straight. If you had told me the whole truth, I would have understood where you were coming from."

"Maybe the whole ugly story about my uncle is something I didn't want to tell anyone, let alone a reporter."

"Dammit, Tess, I'm not just a reporter. I love you. Do you honestly think I would have written about that, knowing how much it would have hurt you?"

"You didn't seem to have any trouble writing that I cheated in the marathon, and that certainly was intended to hurt me," she pointed out.

"That was before I knew about your uncle and what really happened in college," he said softly. "I was real angry, Tess."

"Nick," she gathered her courage in her hands, "how could you love me and not trust me when I told you I had never run in another marathon?"

"How could you love me and not trust me enough to tell me about your uncle?" he countered.

"I never said I loved you," she pointed out carefully.

"No, I guess you didn't," he said after a long pause. "Maybe it was my imagination." He moved a couple of steps closer to her. "Let's check it out and find out if I was wrong."

Before she could move, his arms were around her and his mouth was on hers. For a moment, she furiously tried to push him away, but when his hands moved to her hair and he muttered, "Tess," in a ragged voice, she suddenly collapsed against him.

Desire was like a flash fire that engulfed her whole body. Every place that touched Nick's body cried out for more. She wanted, she needed his fingers and his lips to quench the fire that raged over her. Curling her arms around him, she tried to press even closer.

Her chilled body beneath the damp clothes heated quickly wherever she touched Nick. Heat was radiating from him; she could almost feel it pulsing toward her. She knew she should pull away, stop this now. He was what she needed, though. His arms around her, his mouth on hers were as necessary as breathing.

He smoothed his hands up and down her back, massaging her muscles each time. Cupping her hips in his large palms, he gently squeezed them. When she moaned his name into his mouth, he wrapped his arms around her more tightly than ever.

His mouth was hot and desperate on hers, but her passion matched his. Their mouths caressed, seduced, and demanded until he was trembling as much as she was. When his mouth left hers, it was only to taste her cheek and move down to nuzzle her throat.

His warm breath stirred the hair lying on her neck and made her shiver uncontrollably. Clutching his shoulders, she let head fell back and he slowly moved down to nibble at her collarbones. His tongue traced the outlines of the delicate bones and lingered at the hollow between them.

Somehow her fingers had become entangled in his hair. The wavy strands were slightly coarse as they slipped through her hands. She found the shape of his head fascinating as her fingers lightly roamed over his scalp. When his mouth moved down past her neck, her fingers tightened in his hair.

His mouth pressed kisses on her chest through the thin material of her blouse. The still-damp material was useless as a barrier between his lips and her skin, and every touch of his mouth made her burn even hotter.

One of his hands came around to slowly stroke her stomach and ribs. As he moved with excruciating slowness closer and closer to her breast, his mouth explored the sensitive skin exposed by the V of her blouse. Just when she thought she would scream with frustration, his thumb lightly swept across one of her taut nipples.

Her insides shattered like a pane of glass. Moaning his name, she pressed more tightly against him and felt the hard evidence of his desire for her cradled against her abdomen. She pulled his head down to hers with a soft cry that she didn't even realize she'd made.

Suddenly she was being lifted into the air and Nick was carrying her into her bedroom. When he laid her down on the bed, her mouth was still locked with his, and her arms wrapped around his neck pulled him down on top of her..

The house was completely silent. The only sound she heard was the gentle hiss of the steadily falling rain. It mingled with their unsteady breathing and the murmured endearments that they whispered in each other's ear. The pounding of Tess's heart sounded like thunder and her nerves crackled like lightning. Trying to push her fears to the back of her mind, she let her mouth roam over Nick's face.

His clever, sensitive fingers were unfastening the buttons down the front of her blouse. When the last button opened, he slowly swept the filmy material aside and ran his hand lightly over the exposed skin. Tess shuddered again as his palm rubbed over her nipple, straining against the lacy material of her bra. With a low murmur, he nuzzled his face into the curve of her neck, then slowly nibbled his way downward.

When he reached her bra, he circled her breast, his tongue exploring just inside the edge of the material. Running her hands up his back, she felt his muscles tensed like tightly coiled springs. When he finally flicked his tongue over her waiting nipple, she arched into him and moaned his name. While he was unfastening the clasp of her bra, she unbuttoned his shirt with shaking, unsteady fingers.

Then he was pressing her down into the bed, his weight almost as arousing as his touch had been. The mat of dark hair covering his chest caressed her breasts, tickling them with its springy texture. Nick's face, flushed with passion, poised above hers for an instant. She saw desire and need in his dark blue eyes, now almost black. Searching his face, though, there was something missing. He was holding something back from her, something she needed. He still didn't trust her completely, in spite of the fact that he'd said he loved her.

\*\*\*

He felt the change immediately, and saw it reflected in her eyes in the next instant. She'd pulled away from him, distanced herself, even though their bodies were almost as close as two people could get. He lowered his mouth to hers again, but instead of tasting her desire he felt ashes in his mouth. She wrapped her arms around him, but this time, instead of passion, she was asking for something else, something he didn't know if he could give.

Slowly he eased himself onto his elbows. The separation between them now was more than just that physical distance. She slowly opened her eyes and stared into his for a long moment. What she saw there was apparently not what she wanted to see, because she closed her eyes again, but not before he'd seen the sudden pain in their clear blue depths.

Without a word he sat up and swung his legs over the side of the bed. Tess pushed herself into a sitting position and bent her head to button her blouse. Her blond hair, curling wildly as it dried, swung over her face, hiding it from his view. He watched her silently for a while, then his frustration made him lash out before he could stop himself.

"If you were going to torment me, why didn't you wait until things had gone a little farther?" he said savagely. "It would have been a lot more fun for you than this. We'd barely gotten started."

"Stop, Nick," she whispered. "You know I wanted," her hesitation was painful, "wanted to make love as much as you did."

She looked at him then, and even though her face was flushed red, she watched him steadily. What he saw in her face made his gut twist with fear. Instinctively he turned away from her. No way could he give her what she was asking for. He hadn't given that to a woman in a long, long time. He wasn't even sure he could anymore.

Tess looked at his rigid back and fought to keep the tears from falling. It was only fair, she told herself, if Nick didn't completely trust her. She didn't really trust him either, did she? Even though he had kept his promise to her not to write about the Greener Earth's problems, she couldn't.

Even though he had confronted her about the relationship between her and her uncle instead of just printing it in his column, she didn't dare. When a small part of her brain asked her what else she was waiting for, she ruthlessly pushed it away. Nick wasn't ready to trust her, and that was reason enough.

When she finally slid off the bed and turned to look at Nick, she expected to see anger in his eyes. She wasn't prepared for the pain she saw, but as she reached out instinctively for him, he stood up abruptly. The next instant his eyes were cold and remote, the eyes of some stranger.

He strode into the living room, and Tess followed more slowly. Bending to pick up his discarded sweatshirt, he ran it through his hands almost as if he was nervous. "Tess," he began softly, then stopped. He cleared his throat once, then without meeting her eyes said in an impersonal voice, "Well, if there's anything I can do to help, just let me know." Noticing her bewildered expression, he added, "For the Greener Earth. To help keep it open," he elaborated.

All she could do was stare at him. The Greener Earth was the last thing on her mind. She wanted to yell at him, shake him, do anything to keep him from walking out that door. Remembering the look on his face in the bedroom, she didn't open her mouth. She needed more from him than he was willing to give, and she needed to give him more than she was able to. Maybe it was best this way.

Walking to the door, he opened it and started to leave. Halfway out the door, he turned around and looked back at her. When their eyes met, her heart leaped and she took an involuntary step forward. Then the shutters closed over his eyes again, and the door banged shut behind him. The sound of his footsteps retreated down the wet sidewalk, and moments later his car roared to life and sped away.

Nick clutched the steering wheel tightly, every oath he'd ever heard hissing out through his clenched teeth. He'd never intended for that to happen. *What exactly did you expect?* an irritating voice inside his head asked. He wanted her to admit she loved him and tell him she trusted him. Was that so much to expect? *When you made it plain that you don't trust her?* the voice asked incredulously.

Her face floated in front of him, eyes closed in passion, her lips whispering his name. God, he wanted her so much he ached all over. He'd never wanted a woman the way he wanted Tess Phillips. Remembering how her hands had swept over him and her mouth had tasted him and her body had molded itself to his, he knew that Tess wanted him just as badly. She didn't just want to have sex with him, though. He swallowed but the metallic taste of fear lingered in his mouth. Telling her he loved her wouldn't ever be enough. If he wanted her to give herself to him, he couldn't hold anything back. And he was so afraid of trusting again.

# CHAPTER TEN

"I don't care," Tess yelled into the telephone, "just get that check to us." She slammed down the phone and rubbed her hand over her forehead. She couldn't believe she had actually said that to Will Mahoney. Wearily she picked up the phone to call him back. Even though Will's company owed them some money, that was no reason to bite his head off.

Hanging the phone up with a sigh a few minutes later, she looked up to see Donna standing in front of her desk with a grin on her face and a can of Coke in her hand. "Have you been talking to that deadbeat Mahoney again?"

A reluctant smile quirked the corners of Tess's mouth. "He's only a week late," she admitted. "It doesn't seem to take much to set me off anymore." She sighed again and looked down at the latest bank statement. "I just keep thinking that if I tried harder I could figure out why we're not making enough money."

Donna handed Tess the Coke and flopped down in the chair next to her desk. "So the sorry state of this business is the reason you've been acting like a bear all week?"

"Of course," Tess answered, being careful not to look at Donna. "What other reason could I possibly have?"

"Oh, I can think of one. Six foot three or so, black hair, blue eyes, and a body to die for."

"Nick has nothing to do with this," Tess said firmly, still not looking at Donna. "That interview is history, the column he wrote is history, and Nick Bartholomew is history."

"Is that a fact?" Donna continued to lean back in the chair, watching Tess. "So you're telling me that if he was walking across the yard right now, you wouldn't even bother to look out the window?"

She watched with a grin as Tess practically leaped out of her chair and ran to the window. Sure enough, his familiar figure was striding across the asphalt yard and was almost at the office door. Tess's first panicked reaction was to run and hide in the washroom, but she forced herself to sit back down at her desk. She'd be damned if she would let him think it affected her to see him again.

Her calculator was humming and Tess was busily shuffling papers by the time Nick walked in the door. Donna's muffled chuckling was the only indication that she wasn't deeply immersed in her work.

Donna pushed herself to her feet and ambled off, throwing over her shoulder, "Good luck, Tess, on that history project."

Scowling at Donna, Tess didn't look in Nick's direction. She felt him, though, just standing in the doorway watching her. Every molecule in her body felt his gaze on her, and the memory of the last time she had seen him made her flush with heat. Slowly, almost against her will, she turned to look at him.

He was watching her uncertainly, and for just an instant she saw her yearning reflected in his eyes. Then the moment was gone, and he walked purposefully over to her desk and sat down in the chair Donna had just vacated.

"Tess, I need to talk to you," he said in a low voice.

"What do we need to talk about?" Her eyebrows drew together in a puzzled frown at the secrecy in his voice.

"I need to see the last few months' records from the Greener Earth."

His outrageous demand was stated in such a matter-of-fact voice that Tess could only stare at him. "What did you say?"

"I need to see your records," he repeated impatiently. Hearing his voice rise, he looked around quickly and lowered it again. "You know, the amounts of material you collected, how much you were paid for them, what companies bought them, all that stuff."

Staring at him for a minute, Tess finally shook her head. He seemed perfectly serious. "I think you've been sniffing newsprint too long, Bartholomew. You're talking about *my* company here. Do you seriously think that I'd just meekly hand all my records over to you? To a reporter? To someone who's already ... ?" She stopped and clamped her lips shut. She didn't want to argue about the column again in front of everyone in the office.

"Oh hell, I've done it all wrong." Leaning back in the chair, he ran his hand through his hair. "Listen, Tess, I've been thinking about your problems here. I've had a lot of experience digging up dirt," he had the grace to flush a little, "and I thought that maybe if I took a look at your records I could find something."

All she could do was continue to stare at him. Finally she said in a low voice, "So all you want to do is help me, is that right?" When he nodded and leaned forward, she leaned forward, too, so that their faces were inches apart. "You don't have a follow-up column in mind about Tess Phillips, do you? One where you detail all the problems I'm having here, bolstered by the figures you thought you could wheedle out of me?"

"My God, Tess, do you really think I could do that to you?" His voice was low, but it vibrated with an emotion that Tess was too angry to identify. She ranted on, oblivious to the expression in his eyes.

"Besides, what do you think I've been doing for the last two weeks? Just sitting here wringing my hands and pulling out my hair? I've gone over every number three

153

times, at least, and taken apart every line of this pile of papers." Her hand flew at a stack of documents sitting on her desk, knocking the top few onto the floor. "If I can't find anything wrong, what makes you think you can?"

Standing up abruptly, he pushed the chair back and knocked over a wastebasket. "Sorry, Tess, my mistake." His voice was colder than the most desolate Arctic tundra. "I thought you could use a little help, and I wanted to give you a hand. But I can see that you're doing just fine without me." He yanked the door open, not looking back, and stormed out.

Before he was all the way out the door Tess was half way out of her chair, opening her mouth to call him back. The door shut quietly, carefully, and very finally. Staring at the closed door for a moment, she willed him to open it and walk back in. As the seconds ticked into a minute, she slowly sank back into her chair. Leaning her elbows on her desk, she rubbed both hands over her face.

He was gone for good this time. His face was so utterly cold, so frozen, that she knew it would never thaw. At least, not for her. She'd known the minute the words were out of her mouth that she was wrong. He may not have been able to give her his complete trust, but he did care about her. He'd come here, trying to help her, and she'd said unforgivable things to him. Resting her chin on her hands, she rubbed her eyes. She was so empty inside that there weren't any tears left. Staring out the window, her eyes burned and her heart bled and her soul ached.

\*\*\*

Nick strode angrily across the yard, letting loose with a vicious kick when he saw an empty soda can lying in his path. When it squibbed off the side of his foot, landing a couple of inches away, he picked it up with an oath and hurled it toward the bins fifty feet away. It clattered against the side of the metal container and fell back to the pavement. Just about the same way, he thought bleakly, his anger suddenly gone, that Tess had rejected him.

Climbing into his car, he sat staring blindly out the windshield for a while. After a few minutes, he began to focus on his surroundings. He looked at the bins, where several people were tossing cans and bottles into the large containers. One of the Greener Earth's trucks pulled into the yard, and their logo flashed past him as the truck pulled into the garage. Finally his eyes rested on the office building, its white paint gleaming in the faint November sun.

By God, if Tess wouldn't let him help her, he'd figure out what was wrong on his own. His eyes swept over the scene in front of him again. It had become familiar, and, he realized, important to him over the past few weeks. This business was worth saving, dammit, and he owed her at least that much. Maybe she didn't love him, but she loved her business. If he could figure out what was going on, maybe it would make up for that column that he knew should never have been written. Already planning his strategy, he started the car and sped out of the yard.

\*\*\*

Nick balanced precariously on the closed lid of the toilet, a calculator in one hand and a stack of papers in the other. He passed his arm over his forehead once more. Even though it was a chilly late fall night outside, the closed door of the washroom and the single exposed light bulb illuminating it had turned the small space into a sweatbox. The calculator started to slide off his lap again, and as he grabbed for it the papers fluttered to the floor.

He scooped them up with an oath and leafed through them impatiently until he found the one he was looking for. Holding the calculator steady on both of his knees, he punched the column of numbers into it for the third time. He swore roundly when he saw that the answer was the same as it had been the two times before.

Glancing at his watch, he realized that he'd been sitting in the washroom at the Greener Earth for over three hours. He had looked at every paper sitting on Tess's desk, and as far as he could tell, that meant every paper pertinent to the Greener Earth's financial history. He'd been so certain that he would find some clue to what was happening. Tess was right, he admitted reluctantly. Whatever was going on, the answer wasn't hidden in this stack of papers.

A sudden muscle spasm in his back reminded him that he hadn't stood up in a long time. Turning off the washroom light, he opened the door a crack and peered out. There had been no night watchman lurking in the yard outside when he'd slipped into the building earlier that night. Still, he'd watched the dark, silent yard for a few minutes before opening the door and walking into the office.

The only light in the room was pale splotches of moonlight reflecting off the desks closest to the windows. The rest of the furniture consisted of ghostly lumps and mysterious shapes scattered around the room. Putting his hands on his hips, he stretched his back and felt the bones cracking down his spine. Reaching down to touch his toes, he straightened and sauntered over to Tess's desk.

He grinned as he thought of her reaction if she'd known he was here. Livid would be a mild description, he suspected. There was no point in trying to persuade her to let him look at the records, he'd decided. The word stubborn might have been coined just for her. Instead, he'd taken matters into his own hands and just let himself into the building with the key he knew was kept hidden under a rock.

"Dammit!" he exclaimed out loud as he threw himself into Tess's desk chair. He had been certain that the Greener Earth's financial records would reveal their secrets to him. Instead, he'd wasted three hours and still had no idea what was going wrong.

Scowling, he stared blindly out the window into the yard, thinking. From what Tess had told him, the recycling center had been making a modest profit until about five months ago. Since then, they'd had a bigger and bigger loss each month. By now, they were hanging on through nothing more than willpower. Tess's willpower, he amended grimly.

Finally he stood up, stretched again, and went back into the bathroom for the papers he'd been examining. Replacing them on Tess's desk along with her calculator, his eyes, now accustomed to the darkness, scanned the office to make sure nothing was out of place.

He saw a stack of magazines lying on the floor and had almost dismissed them and moved on when he stopped. Walking over to the untidy pile, he picked up the top magazine and looked at it for a moment. It was a trade journal for the recycling business. Leafing through the pile, he found several months' worth of the same magazine, plus newsletters from various recycling organizations.

Looking around at the slightly untidy office, and remembering the casual atmosphere that seemed to prevail, he suspected that the stack of magazines would never be missed. If someone did look for them, they'd just assume that they were misplaced.

Grinning to himself, Nick picked up the whole collection and stuck them under his arm. Maybe there would be something in one of these magazines that would give him a clue about what could be going wrong. Checking the yard one more time, he slipped out the door, hid the key and hurried out of the yard.

***

Tess aimed the remote control at the television and turned off the pompous anchorman in mid-sentence. The news was depressing, the television drama she'd watched before the news was depressing, and she was certain that whatever was on after the news was bound to be equally depressing. Picking up a paperback bestseller she'd bought just yesterday, she read a few pages before tossing it back on the table.

Her gaze fell on the telephone, and once again she had to stop herself from grabbing it and dialing Nick's number. It had been three days since he'd come to her office, and she'd replayed the scene in her head countless times. Her fingers itched to pick up the phone, call Nick and apologize. But every time she hesitated, her rational self whispered that Nick probably didn't want to talk to her anyway after what she'd said to him three days ago.

She didn't care, she thought suddenly, if Nick wanted to talk to her or not. She owed him an apology for the way she'd treated him. He had come to offer to help her, and she'd lashed out at him because she was hurt. For the past three days, she'd bitterly regretted what she'd said to him, and she wanted to make sure he knew it.

Picking up the phone, she eagerly dialed his number. Her heart pounded in rhythm with each unanswered ring. Finally, when his voice came on the line inviting her to leave a message, she gently replaced the phone in its cradle. So what if he wasn't home at eleven o'clock at night? There were lots of good reasons, she told herself firmly. He was probably at work.

Or maybe, her rational self reminded her, he was out with a woman who was more his type. A woman who was not an athlete and, therefore, inherently more trustworthy. Someone, she thought despairingly, totally different from her.

\*\*\*

When the doorbell rang, Tess was so involved with her own thoughts that she looked around, disoriented. The second, impatient ring had her hurrying to the door. Donna must have forgotten her key again, she thought.

Nick stood at the door, watching her uncertainly. When she merely stared at him, his face hardened and he said abruptly, "I'll only keep you for a minute, Tess, but I need to talk to you."

Somehow she managed to blurt out, "Come in, Nick." She watched as he took off his jacket and hung it on her coat tree, then began, "Nick, I ..."

"Tess, there's ..." he started at the same time. Smiling faintly, he relaxed a little and said, "Go ahead."

Taking a deep breath, she said, "Nick, I'm really sorry about what I said to you at the office the other day. I knew it wasn't true. I was just hurt, I guess, because you didn't trust me. Can you forgive me?"

"Can I forgive you?" He shook his head, incredulity in his eyes. "Tess, sometimes I don't believe you." He stepped in front of her as she started to turn away and gently turned her head so she was forced to face him. "You had every reason not to trust me, and I came barreling in there without a word of explanation, demanding your company records," he said softly. His hands fell to her shoulders, gently kneading them. "I was afraid you'd never forgive *me*."

"What?" she whispered, hope blossoming in her chest.

"I said that I should be the one to apologize, not you," he replied. "Even though," his crooked smile appeared, "you *were* pretty rude. In front of all those people, too. I'm a pretty sensitive guy, you know."

"Yeah, that's what everyone calls you behind your back, Mr. Sensitive Male of the nineties," she said drily. The block of granite in her chest was crumbling. She could feel again, and it was as if she was tingling all over. The heat from his hands on her shoulders was flowing all over her, surrounding her, encircling the two of them.

"Tess," he murmured, his fingers burning her shoulders, his eyes riveted on hers, "are you really going to forgive me that easily?"

"It's not so hard," she whispered, "considering the alternative." If he wasn't ready to trust her she would wait until he was. She had learned, these past few days, that her pride wasn't much of a companion. Nick may not have been ready to trust her completely, but he cared about her enough to want to help her save her business. For now, that would have to be enough.

"The alternative, as you put it, isn't even in the running." Pulling her against him, he muttered into her ear, "God, Tess, I wish we had met any other way than this. I don't know if I'll ever forgive myself for the way I hurt you."

He felt so good, so solid and warm. She didn't ever want to feel as cold again as she had the past three days. Burrowing deeper into his arms, she wrapped her arms around him and held on.

Finally, she stepped back and looked up at him. Cupping his face with both hands, she said firmly, "If we hadn't met like we did, we wouldn't be standing here together now." He opened his mouth, but before he could speak, she hurried on. "You made me realize that I was afraid to get involved with anybody. If I hadn't been forced to spend time with you, I would have sent you packing as soon as I was attracted to you." She grinned and added, "In other words, I would have run screaming into the house the first time we met."

"It's not really that easy, is it, Tess?" he asked gently.

"No, Nick, it isn't. But it's enough for now." Yes, she thought to herself as she lifted her mouth to his, they had all the time in the world to work the rest of it out.

He rubbed his lips lightly along hers, nibbling gently, murmuring her name. Fitting herself into the curve of his body, she knew that this would be how it would feel to return home after a long journey. Back where she belonged.

His mouth on hers was still gentle and undemanding.

It was as if, she thought, he would be content to stand there for hours, rediscovering the texture of her skin, the taste of her lips. She needed more.

Opening her mouth, she traced his lips with her tongue then captured his lower lip with her teeth. His arms tightened around her and he groaned, trying to pull her even closer. Then she couldn't breathe, couldn't think. Nothing in the world mattered except his mouth on hers and his hands roaming over her body.

With shaking hands she pulled the tails of his shirt out of his jeans and slid her palms along his chest. Her fingers tangled in the springy hair, and her thumbs found his flat male nipples. They hardened under her light caresses, making him shudder while he whispered her name into her mouth.

Suddenly the world was spinning, and Nick was carrying her into her bedroom. After laying her on the bed, he sat next to her and watched her while he undressed, his blue eyes smoky and heavy-lidded. Every few seconds he leaned over and kissed her, until by the time he peeled off his briefs and dropped them on the floor, she was shaking as much as he was.

His fingers fumbled as he tried to unfasten the tiny pearl buttons of her blouse. Her nipples tightened in anticipation, and when his hand brushed over her breast she arched into him. As the last button was undone, he spread her blouse and found one nipple with his mouth as he unhooked her bra. Moaning his name, she wrapped herself around him as waves of pleasure broke over her.

Then she tried to unbutton her jeans with hands that shook even as he was trying to pull them over her hips. When they were finally off she tangled her legs with his. The wiry hair on his legs slid over her smooth ones, tickling her everywhere they touched.

He looked down at her, and she pulled his mouth down to hers again.

The heavy length of him pressed down on her, and she

burned with a fire she had never known before. Her hands roamed down his back, caressing his hips and smoothing down the backs of his thighs. His muscles under her hands coiled tighter and tighter until his whole body was trembling.

She was throbbing unbearably. "Nick," she moaned, "I need you. Please ..."

"Oh no, not yet," he whispered into her ear. "I've waited too long for this. I intend to savor every square inch of you."

He lowered his head to nibble her neck while his hand swept down her side. His fingertips skimmed her hips and moved down the inside of her thigh. It felt as if his fingertips were on fire. Every touch of his hand increased the ache inside of her.

His hand smoothed up the inside of her thigh once more and came to rest at the apex of her thighs. When she shuddered convulsively, he crushed her mouth beneath his again, exploring her mouth with his tongue while his hands worked their magic on her body. When she shuddered again and wrapped her legs around him, he whispered into her ear, "Tess, love, open your eyes. I want to watch you while we make love."

His eyes caressed her as he slipped into her. She tightened around him, spiraling higher and higher until she burst over the edge, falling weightlessly through space. At the same time, she felt the tension explode out of Nick's muscles as he gasped her name, over and over.

Nick's weight pressed her down into the mattress, but she held him to her tightly. His face was buried in her hair and his hand rested heavily on her hip. The muscles of his back fascinated her. Her fingers stroked and massaged them until Nick's muffled voice drawled, "Keep doing that and you're asking for trouble."

"I don't think that trouble was exactly what I had in mind," she murmured. She hardly recognized the husky voice as her own.

Still holding on to her, Nick rolled over until she was lying on top of him. "Say that again while I'm looking at you." As a blush stained her cheeks, he grinned. "That's what I thought you said."

Cupping her face in his hands, he brought her head down to his for a swift, hard kiss. "Tell me there's no reason we have to get out of this bed for the next week."

The words were barely out of his mouth when he stiffened, then sat up in bed, pulling her with him. "My God, Tess, I completely forgot why I came here tonight."

Leaning over to nibble his earlobe, she said, "You mean there was another reason?"

His arm around her shoulders tightened and he planted a kiss on her nose. "Get dressed, quick. I'll explain on the way."

Tess leaned back to stare at him. "Let me get this straight. You want me to get dressed? To go out? Right now, at," she glanced at her clock, "one o'clock in the morning?"

Nick was already out of bed, pulling on his jeans. "We have to get over to the Greener Earth tonight. There's no time to explain it to you now, just get dressed."

The urgency in his voice made her slide out of bed and start to throw on her clothes. As he was buttoning his shirt, he glanced over at the silky blouse she'd been wearing and shook his head. "Wear something warmer than that."

As she rummaged through a drawer for a sweater, a thousand different thoughts chased each other through her head. Every possible scenario presented itself, until she was almost frantic with fear. "Just tell me one thing, Nick. Are the buildings still standing?"

Startled, he turned around. When he saw her face, he gathered her into his arms and spoke into her hair. "Sorry, love, I should've known that would scare you. Nothing's wrong, and nothing may happen tonight. I just have some ideas about what's been going on, and we need to be there to keep an eye on things."

They finished dressing quickly and hurried out to Nick's car. The air was cold and the night was clear and silent. Tess watched her breath stream out in front of her as Nick unlocked the car doors. Sitting on the cold leather seat as Nick started the engine, she watched his gloved hands grip the steering wheel and ease the car into the street. It was as if the lateness of the hour and the icy quiet of the night had muffled all sound except her heartbeat in her ears.

"You're not going to like this, Tess," he began. The sound of his voice reverberated in the quiet car. "A few nights ago, I paid a visit to the Greener Earth and looked over all your financial records."

When he glanced at her, as if to gauge her reaction, she raised her eyebrows and said, "You mean you broke into my office?"

He cocked an eyebrow and grinned at her. "Those aren't exactly the words I would choose. I prefer to think of it as creative investigating." When he heard her muffled laugh, he relaxed and grinned at her apologetically. "Believe me, I couldn't think of any other way."

"Well, what did you conclude from your examination of my records?" When he looked her way again, as if he wasn't sure of her reaction, she added gently, "How could I be upset, Nick? I can hardly believe you went to so much trouble for me, especially after what I'd said to you."

Catching her eyes, he pressed a finger to his lips and then to hers. The unexpected, sweet gesture moved her unbearably. Leaning back against the car seat, she took his hand in both of hers and held it on her thigh. They sat that way in silence for the few minutes it took to drive to the Greener Earth.

Nick parked his car around the corner from the entrance and took a heavy blanket, two cushions, and a large thermos out of the back. He took her hand and they walked in silence down the deserted street. When they got to the entrance to the Greener Earth, they ducked under the chain across the driveway and Nick steered her toward the corner of the yard that stood next to the bins and was in deep shadows.

Still without saying a word, he laid the cushions on the ground. After she and Nick sat down, he covered them with the blanket and poured coffee from the thermos. Finally, he said in a low voice, "We're going to wait here until we catch the person who's stealing your material."

She swung her head around to look at him so quickly that the coffee almost sloshed out of the cup. "What do you mean, the person who's stealing our material?"

"It's the only possible explanation for what's been going on here. And if you read those very boring journals about the recycling business that pick up dust on the floor of your office," his crooked grin teased her, "you'd probably have figured it out yourself."

"Can you back up a little and tell me exactly what you're talking about?"

"Well, you were right, you know. The figures on all those papers didn't prove anything except that you weren't making as much money as you used to."

"Thank you," she murmured drily.

"Anyway, just as I was leaving your office, I saw that stack of magazines that you kept on the floor, so on the spur of the moment I decided to take them along and have a look at them." He shook his head and added, "And a very boring three nights I've had, too."

Raising her eyebrows, she murmured, "We'll have to make up for that later." His hands found her under the blanket, and it was quite a while later that she said breathlessly, "I thought we were here to detect."

"No one said we couldn't have fun while we worked," he pointed out. Pulling her back into his arms, he continued, "Anyway, after I read the third or fourth article about the people who are starting to steal recyclables that are left at the curb, I began to wonder. What if someone

165

was doing that here, just on a larger scale? Essentially, waiting for you to collect the stuff, then stealing it before you could sell it."

Frowning, she considered the idea. Finally she shook her head. "That would be practically impossible unless someone that worked here was involved."

"Got it in one," he said with satisfaction.

She turned in his arms to face him. "That's impossible, Nick. No one who worked here would do that. I've known these people for two years, some for a lot longer than that. I know them."

"I can't believe how naive you are, Tess. How much do you really know about any of these people? How do you know what they're really like?"

"I work with these people every day," she said hotly. "I may not be as cynical as you are, but I'm not naive. The people who work here are my friends. They wouldn't steal from me."

"These people are your employees, Tess," he said in a flat voice. "There's a big difference. Look," he said as she started to speak again, "we don't have to argue about this. At least admit there's a possibility that some person, unknown, may be stealing from the Greener Earth." He waited, watching her, until she grudgingly nodded. "Whoever it is, it has to be happening at night. Our only chance to prove what's going on is to catch them in the act. Can we at least agree on that?"

After several moments, she agreed. "It sounds like a possibility, in theory." She watched him as he leaned back and grunted in satisfaction. "So what do we do now?"

"We wait."

# CHAPTER ELEVEN

She was never going to be warm and comfortable again in her life. As Tess arched her back, she could swear her muscles actually groaned in protest. Despite two pairs of socks, her toes tingled with the cold, and she'd long ago given up hope of finding a comfortable place for her legs.

"Do me a favor, will you?" she muttered in a low voice to Nick. "Take a look at my rear end and make sure it's still there. I can't feel a thing."

Nick laughed, squeezing her hand. "I can't believe what a whiner you are, Tess." When she reached out to push him over, he laughed again and used his other hand to pull her into his lap. "Come here. I'll massage it for you." When she grinned in spite of herself, he wiggled his eyebrows and leered, "I'm not sure if it'll help you, but it'll sure make me feel better."

After four nights of camping out at the Greener Earth, she was getting slaphappy. They both were. When Nick turned her over his lap and began kneading the stiff muscles of her buttocks, she laughed so hard she couldn't move. The more she struggled to get away, the harder he massaged and the more she laughed.

Gradually she realized that the pressure of his hands had changed. The brisk massage turned into an intimate caress as his hands smoothed down her legs and traced delicate lines up the insides of her thighs. The cold was forgotten as her heated blood raced through her body. When she turned her head and looked at him, all traces of laughter were gone from his eyes.

"That's odd," he murmured as he drew her up to lay against his chest. "I could've sworn I was cold just a minute ago."

"Must be a heat wave," she whispered just before his mouth came down on hers.

His tongue caressed the velvet softness of her mouth while his hands continued their exploration underneath her down jacket. Her body throbbed with anticipation as she tried to press herself even closer to him. The heavy clothes they both wore, so comforting just a few minutes ago, now seemed like intolerable barriers. Trembling, she fumbled underneath his sweater trying to pull his shirt out of the waistband of his jeans.

He was so hard. Running her hands over the firm planes of his chest, Tess felt him shudder. He was holding all that strength in check with a very fine leash. Her hands curved around and roamed over the corded muscles of his back. When she tore her mouth away from his to suckle his neck, he groaned and rolled her over onto the hard ground.

One of their cushions was under her back and his arm cradled her head. His other hand tugged impatiently at the zipper on the front of her jacket. He was lying half on top of her, with one thigh wedged between her legs. The trembling of his hand as he spread her jacket and his hooded, passion-filled eyes told her that he was as aroused as she was.

The cold air on her heated skin made her gasp as he pulled her sweater up and covered her breast with his mouth. Circling the hard peak with his tongue, he unsnapped her jeans and pulled them down around her hips as she moaned and clasped her legs around him.

Her hands were fumbling with the waistband of his

jeans when she felt him freeze. Her body became perfectly still as she strained to listen. Then she heard a sound, too, a faint clinking, as if someone had moved a chain.

Neither of them moved for what seemed like an eternity. Finally, Nick swung his leg over hers and sat up, then reached down and pulled her into a sitting position. As they buttoned their shirts and tucked them into their jeans, both of them scanned the shadowy yard. The sliver of crescent moon made the metal bins gleam dully, but nothing disturbed the pattern of shadows on the asphalt.

The throb of desire faded as the metallic taste of fear flooded her mouth. She hardly noticed Nick's arm come around her shoulders as she continued to stare into the yard. When they heard the clink again, Nick's arm tightened momentarily before he released her and leaned over to look at the entrance into the yard.

They both heard the footsteps retreating down the sidewalk and the tuneless whistling. As both sounds faded away, Tess let her breath out in a whoosh. Nick rocked back on his heels and said in disgust, "It must have been some kid unhooking the chain across the entrance. Doesn't he have anything better to do at one o'clock in the morning?"

Tess strained to hear, but the footsteps had faded away completely and once again the street was deserted. Turning to Nick, she said, "Are you sure we don't have something better to do at one o'clock in the morning?"

Pressing a hard kiss on her mouth, Nick replied, "Don't worry, I have lots of plans. You'll just have to use your imagination until after we catch our thief."

"Nick, I appreciate the fact that you're trying to help me. We've sat out here all night for four nights, though, and there's been no sign of anyone prowling around. Maybe we need to think about some other way to catch whoever's doing this."

Leaning back against the wall, he stretched his long legs out in front of him. "Do you still agree that someone is probably stealing from you?"

Turning to face him, she nodded slowly. "It does seem to be the only answer that makes any sense. I'm just not sure that this is the way it's being done."

He leaned forward to drop a kiss on her nose. "Believe me, sweetheart, this is not my first choice of how to spend my nights, either. I can think of all kinds of things I'd rather be doing." His husky voice and smoky eyes made her tingle. "In fact, I ..."

His hand tangled in her hair and his lips were poised above hers when the sound of a car driving into the yard drowned out the rest of his words. Both of them spun around to look, but the car had driven behind the bins, and in order to see it they would have had to walk into the open.

After a few moments, they heard the rumble of one of the garage doors being opened, and one of the collection trucks roared out of the yard. As soon as the truck went past them, Nick and Tess dashed across the yard and out of the recycling center. The taillights of the truck were two blocks away and getting smaller.

"Watch the truck!" Nick yelled at her as he began to run down the street. "I'll get the car."

The red lights were pinpoints when Nick's car roared up and slowed down just enough for her to jump in. Without taking her eyes off the red points of light ahead, she said, "He's still up there. Hurry!"

Nick stamped on the gas pedal and the acceleration slammed her back into her seat. The truck was moving slowly, because the red lights got steadily larger. When they pulled within two blocks of the truck, Nick abruptly slowed down. Tess glanced at him questioningly, and he smiled grimly. "We don't want him to know we're following him. Might as well catch everyone who's involved."

His icy tone made Tess shiver, and she looked at the truck again. If whoever was in there hadn't been stealing from her, she could almost feel sorry for him. She was devoutly glad Nick wasn't chasing her with that look on his face.

Nick kept the truck within two or three blocks of his car, and the driver apparently had no idea he was being followed. He drove along steadily, occasionally making a turn but making no effort to elude them. When Tess finally looked out their window to see where they were, she frowned. "This doesn't make any sense," she exclaimed.

Nick glanced at her quickly, then looked back out the windshield. "What?"

"We're heading out into the country. There's nothing out here except farms and a forest preserve. I guess I just assumed that they'd be taking the stuff to some company that buys recyclables, but there's nothing like that out here."

He shrugged. "He's got to be going somewhere. When he gets there, we will, too."

They drove for ten more minutes, exchanging few words. Nick reached for her and rested their joined hands on her thigh. Every so often he gave her a reassuring squeeze, and finally said softly, "Don't worry, love. This is the easy part."

"Is it?" she murmured.

He looked away from the road long enough to give her a puzzled frown. "What do you mean?"

Staring at the red lights in front of them, she didn't answer for a minute. Finally, she said, "Whoever's in that truck is probably someone I know, Nick. Someone I work with every day, someone I've joked with. Someone that I think of as a friend." She turned in her seat so she was facing him. "The betrayal of that friendship is much worse than the money they've been stealing from me. Money is nothing. I don't have a family I can count on, so I counted on my friends. And one of them is ruining my business, which was the only other thing that was important to me."

He released her hand and gently brushed her hair back from her face. "As soon as I realized what had to be happening, I knew it had to be someone from the Greener Earth. I'm sorry, Tess. People can be rotten sometimes."

"Not my friends, Nick!

"I hope not, sweetheart," he murmured. His hand brushed protectively over her face, then dropped down to capture her hand again.

They followed the red dots in front of them in silence for a few more minutes. Then Tess said suddenly, "Slow down! He's going to turn."

By the time they reached the spot where the truck had turned, it was nowhere in sight. Nick pulled the car onto the shoulder of the road as they both stared, puzzled, at the sign next to the road.

"What the hell is a recycling truck doing in a forest preserve?" Nick said.

"He's got to be either meeting someone or dumping something," Tess answered slowly. When Nick quirked his eyebrows at her, she explained. "There's no other exit from this forest preserve besides this one. This was where I ran when I did my long runs before the marathon, and I tried to go through it once."

He stared at the entrance for a moment, then drove his car up the road and turned it around. When he parked on the shoulder, he turned to Tess and said, "If anyone comes along, we're just a parking couple." Running his fingers through her hair, he leaned closer. "Think you can handle that?"

Staring at the forest preserve entrance, she reached out and took his hand. "I'm sure we could convince anyone that was interested."

Every minute that ticked past seemed like an hour. Twice Tess reached out and wiped away the condensation that fogged the window. Finally they heard the rumble of a truck approaching the entrance. Tess reached for her seat belt and fastened it then leaned forward in her seat, wiping the window again. As the truck turned slowly onto the road, she frowned. When it had pulled away from them and started to pick up speed, she turned to Nick. "That wasn't our truck," she exclaimed.

He was writing on a scrap of paper. "I know. It must belong to whoever's buying the stuff. I couldn't see his license plate real clearly, but I got some of the letters. Maybe we can trace it from that."

"Why bother to come all the way out here? There must be a lot of other places they could meet."

"There aren't any prying eyes out here, Tess," Nick answered grimly. "My guess would be that they didn't want to take a chance on someone spotting one of your trucks where it wasn't supposed to be. It's dark enough out here to hide a lot of things."

"Here comes the other truck," she interrupted him. They both watched intently as a second truck rolled onto the road. "That's ours," she confirmed.

Nick let it get a couple blocks ahead of them, then started the car and followed. "My guess would be that he's headed back to the Greener Earth."

They followed the truck along the same route they had taken out into the country. Before long they were driving through the silent streets of Oak Ridge toward the Greener Earth. When it became obvious that the truck was going back to the recycling center, Tess's already jittery stomach began to churn.

By the time they pulled into the yard behind the truck, her arms and legs were trembling and her stomach was roiling with nausea. She took a deep breath and unclenched her hands from the sides of her seat. Whatever happened, it would be over soon. And Nick was with her.

The car had barely stopped when she was out the door and running. Behind her, Nick swore, jumped out of the car and pocketed his keys before he ran after her. "Tess, wait for me." She didn't even look around at the low sound of his voice. *Please, God*, she prayed, *let it be a stranger*.

Just as she reached the truck, the door opened and a shadowy figure swung down. The pool of light from the inside of the truck illuminated his face perfectly. Tess stopped, only dimly aware of Nick coming up behind her.

For a moment Tess and the man standing next to the truck could only stare at each other. The man was the first to speak. "Well, I guess the game's up, isn't it, Tess?"

She said softly, "How could you, Mike?"

"It was real easy, Tess. This place was going under anyway. I was just making sure I got my share."

"We were doing fine until you started stealing from us!" she cried.

"Yeah, well I guess our definitions of 'fine' are a little different. As far as I'm concerned, the pittance we're getting out of this place is not 'fine.' "

"There are other people who work here, Mike. They're friends of yours, too. They need their paychecks. What are they supposed to do when we have to close?"

He shrugged dismissively. "There are other jobs."

"I thought that this business was as important to you as it was to me. I thought you were as concerned about the environment as I was."

Laughing, he shook his head. "Boy, Tess, you are something else. The only thing that's important to me is Mike Borgren. When I finally realized that your uncle wasn't going to cave in and start pouring money into this place, I knew it was time to get my share and get out. I stuck around here for two years, and I figure I deserve everything I got."

Tess had almost forgotten about Nick standing behind her. When he brushed past her, she jumped. Grabbing Mike by the collar, he snarled, "You deserve everything you get, all right, Borgren." There was a sickening crunch as Nick's fist connected with Mike's face. "Exactly how much did you have in mind?"

Nick managed to land three more blows before he noticed that Tess had grabbed his arm. "Stop, Nick," she repeated, over and over, until his arm dropped and he stepped away from Mike. Wrapping her arms around him, she said fiercely, "Don't! He's not worth it!"

Without taking his eyes off Mike, he said grimly, "All right, Tess, I promise I won't touch him while you go call the police. But you better hurry before I change my mind."

Tess held onto him and said, "I'm not going to call the police. I just don't want to see him again. As long as he's gone, the business has a chance to survive, and that's what's important to me. Just let him go, Nick."

"You are kidding, aren't you?" Nick asked incredulously. "You're not really serious?"

"Of course she is," Mike broke in scornfully. "You ought to know her by now. Tess is too pure and noble to turn me over to the police. I had that figured out, too."

With an oath, Nick pried her arms away and leaped at Mike. Grabbing him by the collar, he shook him until he was limp in his hands. "She may want to let you go, buddy, but don't think you're getting off that easily. You and I have some business to discuss."

Holding Mike by the back of his coat, Nick dragged him to the office. Fifteen minutes later, Mike emerged and walked slowly to his car without another glance at Tess. She jumped out of the truck, where she'd been looking through the papers Mike had left there, and walked toward the office.

When she walked in the door, Nick rose from her desk chair. "How could you let him go after what he did to you?" he asked abruptly.

"It's not that black and white, Nick," she sighed. "If it hadn't been for Mike, I wouldn't have been able to start this business in the first place. Besides, the publicity we'd get if I had him arrested would probably accomplish what

Mike was trying to do. I just couldn't take the chance."

He scowled at her for a minute, then a reluctant smile curved his lips. "Well, I can see you didn't learn anything from your uncle about running a business." The smile grew wider as he added, "Thank goodness."

Something shifted inside Tess. It was as if, with two simple sentences, Nick had realigned her thinking. If Nick saw the differences between her and her uncle so clearly and, just as clearly, came down on her side, then perhaps the problem was with her uncle, not her. Could it really be that simple?

Oblivious to Tess's dazed look, Nick picked up some papers from her desk and waved them at her. "You may have wanted to let him go, but I didn't think you wanted him to be any part of the Greener Earth." At her questioning look, he explained. "These papers give you complete ownership of Mike's half of the Greener Earth, in exchange for your promise not to prosecute him for the thefts that have gone on for the past five months."

"What?" she gasped.

"You don't want him waltzing back in here six months or a year from now, just when you're starting to get back on your feet, and ask for his share of the business. By then all the proof would be gone, and legally there wouldn't be a thing you could do." Looking down at the papers, he continued. "At least you can be sure that he's not going to show up here again. If what you wanted was to be rid of Mike Borgren, you've got it."

"Nick," she said slowly, "thank you. You're right, I wasn't thinking past today." She paused, then added, "I know you don't agree with me. One part of me would like nothing better than to see him locked up. It's better for the Greener Earth, and for me, though, to do it like this. I need to put this behind me, and everything involved with arresting him would only make it worse."

"I know," he said simply. "He was your friend, and in jail he would be a constant reminder of how he betrayed you."

She smiled shakily at him, and pressed a quick kiss on his mouth. "Let me see those papers," she finally murmured.

Nick sat on the edge of her desk with his legs crossed, swinging one foot, as she began to read. Her stomach twisted as she read Mike's description of how much and how often he had stolen from the company. Clenching her teeth, she forced herself to read everything he had written.

Without any warning, Nick jumped off her desk and exclaimed, "I almost forgot! Tess, I have to run. I can't explain now. 'Bye."

Leaning back in her chair, Tess watched Nick dash out the door without a backward look. A few seconds later, his car roared to life and sped out of the yard. She listened for a few minutes, sure that he would turn around and come back. When she finally acknowledged that he was gone, she slumped back in her chair and stared, unseeing, out the window.

Was this Nick's way of saying good-bye? Did he feel that he'd paid his debt to her and could leave now with his conscience clear? No, she told herself sternly, she trusted Nick and believed that he loved her. He would be back.

# CHAPTER TWELVE

B y the next afternoon she wasn't so sure. After waiting at the Greener Earth for an hour the previous night, she'd finally called Donna to come and get her. She and Donna had stayed up most of the night, talking about what had happened and what to do next at the Greener Earth. The next morning, emotionally drained and physically exhausted, Tess had insisted on going back to her office to explain everything to her co-workers. Now, at one o'clock in the afternoon, she was so tired she was barely capable of putting two thoughts together. And Nick still hadn't called.

Abruptly she spun around in her chair. "Donna, I have to go home," she said quietly.

"Go ahead," Donna answered. "I've got things under control here. What should I tell the bas ... er, Nick, in case he calls?"

"I don't care," she answered wearily. "I'm not even sure what my name is, let alone what I want you to tell Nick."

"Good."

Tired as she was, Tess recognized the note in Donna's voice. "Donna ..." she warned.

"Don't worry, I won't say anything you wouldn't say yourself if you were in any condition to talk."

Walking out the door, Tess gave a small laugh. "Now, why doesn't that reassure me?"

When she finally got home, she stripped off the clothes she'd been wearing for almost twenty four-hours and left them lying on the floor. Checking her answering machine one more time, just to make sure she hadn't overlooked a flashing red light, she fell into bed. Her last conscious thought was of Nick. She was trying to hold onto him, but he kept moving farther and farther away. As she reached out for him one last time, he faded away completely.

*\*\*\**

She drifted slowly out of the soft cocoon of sleep. There was something wrong, she knew, but she couldn't quite put her finger on it. As she opened her eyes, the darkness of the room disoriented her. It seemed like there should be daylight outside the window. Sitting up and pushing the hair out of her eyes, the first thing she saw was the pile of clothes on the floor. Frowning, she glanced at the clock. Four o'clock in the morning. Then she looked at the telephone, and everything came flooding back. Mike. The Greener Earth. And Nick, who hadn't called.

Leaning back against the headboard of the bed, she thought about Nick. It had been almost twenty-four hours since he walked out the door at the Greener Earth. Surely there had been a couple of minutes in that time when he could have picked up the phone and called her. Maybe she'd been right the first time. Maybe he wasn't coming back.

Throwing back the covers, she wondered numbly why she didn't feel anything. If she was lucky, she told herself, she wouldn't feel anything for a long, long time. She grabbed a robe and wandered into the kitchen for a glass of water. There had to be something else she could think about besides Nick Bartholomew.

The trouble was, at four o'clock in the morning her

mind tended to focus right on the basic issues. No matter how hard she tried to think about something else, Nick's face kept appearing in front of her eyes. The empty ache inside her seemed to grow and grow, until nothing else in the world existed. No matter how hard she tried to erect walls, there was finally nothing left as a barrier between her and her grief.

Leaning against the kitchen counter, all she could think about was Nick. Jogging steadily along beside her, even though she knew his lungs were ready to burst. Interviewing the football player who'd been cut from the team and seeing through the swagger to the man's pain. Kissing her.

The tears she couldn't shed lodged like a stone in the back of her throat. Her eyes were so dry they burned. She needed to cry, but she was empty. All her tears were locked away, trapped in the rock that made it difficult to breathe, impossible to swallow. Later, she knew, she would cry enough tears for a lifetime. For now, she could only ache.

The hands of the clock moved with excruciating slowness. It was still totally black outside. Restlessly she pushed away from the kitchen counter and paced into the living room. That was no better. Instead of seeing Nick sitting at her kitchen counter drinking coffee, she saw him sprawled on her couch. The bedroom would be infinitely worse, she was afraid.

She could call him, she told herself. After all, this wasn't the middle ages. It was perfectly acceptable to call a man. No, she told herself fiercely. He walked out on her. She wasn't going to crawl to him. She'd done enough of that in her life with her uncle. She was done with crawling.

Abruptly she walked into her bedroom and rummaged in a dresser drawer, looking for her running clothes. She needed to run. If she ran far enough, fast enough maybe it would erase him from her mind. Dressing quickly, she stepped outside. For a while, anyway, she could run away from him.

\*\*\*

The bitterly cold wind cut through her sweatshirt and her stomach muscles clenched. It whipped at her face, making her nose numb and her eyes water. Her legs pounded relentlessly on the pavement. The numb, mindless state of total physical exhaustion was getting closer. She turned down another street and changed directions, heading for home. If she was lucky, she could shower, get dressed and be at work before her mind started functioning again. There was enough there to keep her mind occupied for the rest of the day. She refused to think beyond that.

The spare light of a November dawn was spreading over the sky when she turned into her driveway. Gasping and shaking, covered with sweat in spite of the cold, she stumbled to her front door. With the door half way open, her foot kicked the wrapped copy of the Chicago Post that lay on the porch. Automatically, only half looking at it, she bent over to pick it up. Her hand was half way to the ground when she froze.

Lying on top of the folded paper was a single red rose. She stared at it for a long moment before bending all the way down and picking it up. The heavy, seductive scent surrounded her, intensified by the sharp, cold air. Hope swept through her in an instant, making her look around eagerly. However, the street was just as deserted as it had been when she'd run down it a few minutes ago.

Glancing around one last time, Tess turned to walk into the house. Almost as an afterthought she bent to retrieve her newspaper. Still staring at the rose, she dropped the paper on the living room floor and sat down on the couch. She was still sitting there, the rose held delicately between two fingers, when the doorbell rang.

As she walked across the floor, her heart started

pounding harder than it did when she ran. By the time she opened the door, her heart was racing so fast it threatened to suffocate her. Nick stood there with another red rose in his hand.

She wasn't sure how long she'd been staring at him when he finally said, "Tess? Can I come in?" Something about his subdued tone made her blink her eyes and really look at him. She'd never heard that tone in his voice before.

"Oh, ah, sorry, Nick. Come on in." As she stepped aside, he brushed against her arm. The heat started there and swept through her body. She gripped the doorknob tightly and held it for a moment before shutting the door. Swallowing hard, she followed him across the room and sat down in a chair opposite him.

It was the first time, she realized, that she had seen Nick at a loss for words. He just sat there, staring at her, unnerving her more with each passing second. Finally, unable to bear the tension a moment longer, she blurted, "Thank you for the rose," then kicked herself mentally for being so trite.

Her obvious nervousness seemed to make him relax. Leaning back into the cushions of the couch, he answered softly, "You're welcome, love." Twirling the stem that he still held, he seemed to take pity on her as he leaned forward and held the other rose out to her. "Why don't you put them in some water?"

She was more than happy to retreat into the kitchen. A few minutes alone was what she needed to regain her composure. After arranging the two roses in a bud vase, she took a deep breath and walked slowly back into the living room.

Before she could sit back down in the chair, Nick jumped up and guided her to the couch next to him. Her pulse jittered at his touch, and she moved just a hair farther away from him. Slowly, as if he was afraid that she would pull away, Nick took her hand. Lacing his fingers with hers, he cradled her hand in both of his.

"I'm sorry I didn't call yesterday," he began abruptly. "There was something I had to do before I could talk to you again."

"What was that?" she whispered hoarsely.

Instead of answering, he stood and picked up her morning newspaper from where she'd dropped it on the floor. Pulling off the plastic wrapper, he flipped through the sections until he found the one he was looking for. He walked back to the couch and handed her the sports section without saying a word.

The first thing she saw was his picture at the top of the page. Without glancing at him, she began to read his column.

After the first paragraph she looked up, but Nick had moved over to gaze out the window. She stared at him wonderingly for a moment, then read the rest of the column. Finally, her eyes glittering with unshed tears, she looked over at him standing by the window. He watched her uncertainly, as if he were unsure of her reaction.

"Nick," she whispered. "My love, you didn't have to do this for me."

At that he came over and sat next to her again. "I had to do it for me," he said quietly. "I couldn't have looked you in the eye again if I hadn't set the record straight. It was long overdue, Tess."

"I know you don't think I lied or cheated to win the marathon. You didn't have to say you were," she looked down at the column again, "a 'blind, stupid fool not to have seen all along what a champion Tess Phillips was.' " She smiled a little and touched his cheek. "Especially in such a public way."

"I slammed you in a public way in my first column, so I thought it was only fair that I make my apologies in the same way."

"But you make me sound like some kind of heroine," she protested. "I'm not a 'winner all the way through;' I'm just an ordinary person who has a talent for running. The way you talk about all my victories in college, you make me sound like some sort of, of, legend in the making or something. That's not really me you're talking about."

"Oh, yes, it is. If you don't make the next Olympic marathon team, it'll only be because you didn't try out." When she opened her mouth to contradict him, he put his finger over her lips. "You're that good, Tess, and you know it." Leaning toward her, he took her by the shoulders and said slowly. "The only person you have to prove anything to is Tess Phillips. And the only person you'll be disappointing if you don't succeed is yourself. It's that simple, Tess, and it always has been."

The only thing she could do was stare at him. "How do you know ..."

When she stumbled to a halt, he finished, "How do I know what your uncle did to you? I'm a reporter, remember? That's what I'm supposed to do. When I wrote that first column, I just forgot that you're supposed to get the information first and then write the story." His hand weaved through her braided hair. "I tried to get it right this time."

"Just one more thing," she murmured without taking her eyes off him. "Who's Vicky Chessman and what does she have to do with me?" She didn't have to look at the words to remember them. "Tess Phillips is not another Vicky Chessman and never could be. I was just too dumb to realize that until it was almost too late."

"Vicky," he said softly, "is ancient history." When Tess just watched him, he sighed. "She was a pro tennis player. What she lacked in talent she more than made up for in cunning. Unfortunately, I was too infatuated with her to realize that. By the time I realized that she was only pretending to be madly in love with me in order to get me to write glowing columns about her, we were engaged. Ever since," he flashed his crooked grin, "I've had kind of an attitude about women athletes."

Her answering grin faded as she saw the tenderness in his eyes. Putting her arms around his neck, she laid her head on his chest and burrowed in. "I was so scared," she confessed. "I wanted so badly to trust you, but when you didn't call, I just assumed that you weren't going to." She looked up at him, and the tears that had been threatening since she read his column dripped slowly down her face. "Can you forgive me for not trusting you?"

Wrapping his arms tightly around her, he said in a low growl, "It's not like you have a lot of practice with someone being there for you."

"No," she agreed quietly. "My uncle didn't teach me much about loving someone. You've done that, Nick."

Running his thumbs over her face, he wiped away her tears. When she reached up to touch his face, he brushed her lips with his. Tess could feel how tightly he held himself in check in order to be gentle. As his lips brushed hers again, desire crashed over her like a wave. Fierce and powerful, it was anything but gentle. Pulling his mouth down to hers, she opened her mouth and poured herself into him.

His arms crushed her to him as his mouth devoured hers. "Oh, God, Tess," he moaned into her mouth. As her hands unbuttoned his shirt, he pulled the elastic band from her braid and teased her hair loose.

Somehow they ended up on the floor. Tess didn't remember moving off the couch. The only thing she felt was Nick's hands touching her, exploring everywhere, claiming her for his own. All she tasted was his passion, mixed with her own, a dark, rich flavor that swirled in her head. Then his hands slid under her sweatshirt and found her breasts, teasing the nipples into hard peaks and making her moan his name as she arched into him.

"Tess," his voice rasped in her ear. "I need to hear you." His tongue flicked into her ear, making muscles deep inside of her tremble. "Do you want me, Tess?"

"Ah, Nick," she moaned as he bent his head to her

bared breasts. "I've waited for you for so long. You're all I'll ever want."

She slipped her hand inside the waistband of his jeans and smoothed her palm over his firm buttocks. At her touch, he tensed, and as her other hand moved over his back, she felt how tightly he was coiled, how hard he was trying to hold himself in check.

When she squeezed his hips gently and felt him shudder, her own body spiraled tighter in response. Her hands were clumsy with her haste as she searched for the snap of his jeans, then tugged them impatiently over his hips. As he peeled them off, she pulled his shirt over his head without bothering to unbutton it.

She pressed herself against his naked body, her mouth roaming over him greedily. She needed to taste and savor every inch of his hard, muscled body.

Nick captured her hands and held them against his chest. His heart felt like a piston slamming against her fingers. "Tess," he whispered hoarsely, "there's something wrong with this picture." When she looked up at him in surprise, he lowered his mouth to hers for a desperate kiss. "As sexy as I find your sweatpants and sweatshirt," he muttered into her mouth, "you're definitely overdressed for this party."

His hands slid the loose pants over her hips and swept them off. Her sweatshirt followed, and suddenly he rolled her onto her back and wedged himself between her thighs, whispering her name. She reached for him as her own passion spiraled out of control. They moved together, driven by desperate need, until she cried out and arched into him. He gasped her name one more time as his whole body convulsed.

They laid on the floor, their arms and legs wrapped around each other, gasping and trembling. Finally Nick eased himself onto his side and pulled Tess into his arms again. His breath tickled her ear and lifted her hair. "Can I take this to mean that you've forgiven me?"

Smiling up at him, she traced the line of his cheek down to his chin and let her finger smooth over his lips. "I don't know, which offense are we talking about here?" she murmured mischievously.

In answer he rolled her onto her back again and tickled her unmercifully. As she squirmed against him, giggling and laughing, she couldn't help notice how aroused he was becoming. She put her hands up to cup his face as he stopped tickling her and let his fingers trail down to her thighs. Looking steadily into his deep blue eyes, she said slowly, "I love you, Nick. I can't ..."

The rest of her words disappeared into his mouth as he pressed his lips against hers in a passionate kiss. Finally his lips trailed to her ear, nibbling as he moved along. "I love you, too, Tess." Supporting himself on his elbows, he pushed her hair back from her face and looked down at her. "Tell me again."

"I love you. I love you. I love ..." Once more, her words were choked off by his lips. When she could breathe again, she said, "I'm going to tell you how much I love you until you get sick of hearing me say it. If I hadn't been so frightened of my feelings for you, I would have told you a lot sooner."

"Is that so?" he grinned. "You sure you're just not lusting after my magnificent body? 'One set of hormones calling out to another set of hormones' is the phrase that comes to mind."

"I don't know," she answered. The note of concern in her voice contrasted with the twinkle in her eyes. "But you know what they always say."

"What's that?" he murmured against her neck.

"You should always put your theories to a practical test." Running her hand down his side and around to his thigh, she whispered, "Do you know of any way to be sure?"

"No, I don't," he said as he kissed his way down her neck, "but right now I don't care. I'll take you any way I can get you." Raising his head, he grinned down at her. "Any time, any place, anyhow."

As her arms wrapped around his neck, he scooped her up and carried her into the bedroom.

A long time later, Tess opened her eyes and looked at Nick's face lying next to hers on the pillow. Dark stubble shadowed his cheeks and chin and his thick black eyelashes laid against his skin. As if he was aware of her scrutiny, his eyes slowly opened. When they focused on her face, he gave her a lazy smile and reached out his arm to pull her next to him.

"So tell me, love, when are you going to marry me?"

"I wasn't aware that I'd been asked."

Pulling away from her, he looked at her with feigned astonishment. "Are you sure I didn't fall down on my knees and beg you to marry me the first time I saw you in those baggy sweatpants and sweatshirt?"

Grinning at him, she said, "That bad, huh?"

"Yup. That's when I knew I was a goner. I kept imagining what those shapeless clothes were hiding. They were responsible for more than one restless night. Of course, once I found out, I couldn't sleep at all."

She had never known she could be so happy. "How about if I just give you the sweats?"

"No way." He pulled her back against him. "I'll consider nothing less than a package deal." He kissed her thoroughly, then held her away from him.

The grin was gone from his eyes as he said seriously, "I'll still find your body incredibly exciting when you're ninety years old, but that's not why I want to marry you, Tess. I love the person inside of that body."

Raising himself on his elbows, he stroked her hair and said, "I love your idealism and your sincerity. I've never known anybody so trusting or so giving. You've given me so much that it scares me. I don't know if I can ever give as much back to you."

"Nick," she murmured, touching his face, "you've

already given me more than I could ever possibly give you. You've taught me to trust my feelings again. After the way I failed with my uncle, I wasn't even sure I knew how to love anyone. Or that anyone could ever love me."

"Your uncle," he said roughly, "is a fool. Not only that, he's a stupid fool." Wrapped tightly in his arms, they held each other without speaking for a few minutes.

"You know," he said finally, "it's all right with me, but the children might not like it."

"What are you talking about?"

"Not getting married. If you just want to live together, I guess I could go along with that, but once the kids get a little older, they might think it's kind of funny. You know, why their parents aren't married when all the other kids' parents are."

"Silly ass," she murmured against his chest. "Of course, I'm going to marry you." Looking up at him, her eyes suspiciously bright, she added, "We wouldn't want to do anything to embarrass the kids."

Smiling down at her, he mused, "Of course, they're going to be embarrassed enough about the way we carry on in public. What's one more little family disgrace?"

"One too many," she said firmly.

Tess pressed closer to him. All that was left was to tell him again how much she loved him. She didn't think she could ever find the exact words, but she had a whole lifetime to try.

*****

# ABOUT THE AUTHOR

Margaret Watson has always made up stories in her head. When she started actually writing them down, she realized she'd found exactly what she wanted to do with the rest of her life. More than twenty years after staring at that first blank page, she's an award-winning, two-time RITA finalist who has published thirty books for Harlequin. She has recently embarked on a career as an indie publisher, and the first three books in her new Donovan Family series are now available.

When she's not writing or spending time with her family, she practices veterinary medicine. Although she enjoys that job, writing is her passion.

Margaret lives in a Chicago suburb with her husband and three daughters and a menagerie of pets

She loves hearing from her readers. Contact her at margaret@margaretwatson.com, or check out her Facebook page, Margaret Watson Author. Visit her website at http://www.margaretwatson.com.

Made in the USA
Monee, IL
16 April 2025

15900690R00114